"There's just one more thing," Eric said.

Kit paused. "What?"

"Kiss me, Kit."

In the next moment Eric was pulling her to him, kissing her gently but thoroughly. And she kissed him back, enjoying the moment. That was all anyone could ever count on, wasn't it? The moment. Kiss me, Kit. The words sang in her mind and she listened to them, memorizing their melody.

Dear Readers,

We at Silhouette would like to thank all our readers for your many enthusiastic letters. In direct response to your encouragement, we are now publishing *four* FIRST LOVEs every month.

As always FIRST LOVEs are written especially for and about you—your hopes, your dreams, your ambitions.

Please continue to share your suggestions and comments with us; they play an important part in our pleasing you.

I invite you to write to us at the address below:

Nancy Jackson
Senior Editor
Silhouette Books
P.O. Box 769
New York, N.Y. 10019

KISS
ME, KIT!
Dorothy Francis

First Love from Silhouette

Published by Silhouette Books New York

America's Publisher of Contemporary Romance

First Loves by Dorothy Francis

New Boy in Town (#1)
Special Girl (#8)
Say Please! (#20)
A Secret Place (#27)
Just Friends (#41)
Kiss Me, Kit (#82)

 SILHOUETTE BOOKS, a Division of Simon & Schuster, Inc.
1230 Avenue of the Americas, New York, N.Y. 10020

Copyright © 1984 by Dorothy Francis

Distributed by Pocket Books

ISBN: 0-671-53382-7

First Silhouette Books printing February, 1984

10 9 8 7 6 5 4 3 2 1

America's Publisher of Contemporary Romance

Printed in the U.S.A.

1

Kit Cummings locked her suitcase and set it beside the door of her hospital room. She paced, trying to walk without limping, trying to forget the previous February's car crash that had landed her first in Miami General Hospital and then in the Dade County rehabilitation center where she had been for four long months. The memory was like a kaleidoscope of scary scenes. Now the nightmare was almost over. But was a new nightmare starting?

What if she would always need to wear the built-up shoe on her left foot? Even if her chinos almost hid it, she knew it was there. What if her leg never regained its full strength? But most important of all, what if she weren't strong enough to pole the *Sea Sprite* across the backwaters for gramp that summer? She squared her shoulders, knowing that if she held herself straight she was almost five feet nine inches tall. She needed all the height she could get. Tall people could spot fish from a boat's poling platform more easily than short people. She had to stand tall. And she had to be strong, too. *She had to be*.

Backwater fishing in the keys was her life. It was going to be her profession once she finished her senior year at Key West High School. She tried to tell herself she would grow strong during the summer. She just felt weak then because everyone had babied her, treated her like a hothouse orchid. But she was through with wheel chairs and crutches. She was ready to step out and do things on her own.

How she would welcome leaving that room! Green walls. Green curtains. Green floor. Were all hospital rooms so green? There was even a green smell about it. She smiled at that thought. Who ever heard of a green smell! When she had complained about the color, the nurses had just laughed and pointed out that the walls matched her eyes.

"How are you doing, Kit?" Nurse Yankton stepped into the room, her white nylon uniform carrying the medicinal scent of camphor and rubbing alcohol. "Is there anything I can do to help you get ready to greet your parents?"

"Negative, Nancy." Kit grinned down at the short wiry woman, her favorite of all the nurses at the clinic. "I'm ready to go." She pushed her scuba gear closer to the door.

"I'd give my nurse's cap for neat scuba gear like that," Nurse Yankton said. "Well, almost, anyway. You're really lucky to have such a thoughtful grandfather."

"I'd give the stuff to you if I could," Kit said. "But gramp would be hurt. "I'd hate him to guess that I'm not interested in it."

"Really?" Nancy asked. "You really care nothing about scuba diving?"

Kit shook her head. "Learning the routines in the pool was good therapy for my leg, and it helped me fill lots of dead minutes here at the clinic, but I don't plan to go in for deep-sea diving once I'm home. Fishing's my thing, Nancy. I can hardly wait to board gramp's boat, to pole onto the flats, to watch for those knuckles in the waves that tell me there's a permit or a bonefish skimming just beneath the surface."

"Whatever turns you on," Nurse Yankton said, smiling. Then she picked up a card from Kit's bedside table. "Don't forget this. Looks like your report card."

"Right. It is. I want to show it to my folks first thing. They've been so worried about my completing my school year, passing the finals and all. Dad's a math teacher at high school, and mom's a librarian. They're scholarship oriented."

"You lucked out, being able to finish your junior year by correspondence," Nurse Yankton said. "Care if I take a peek at your grades?"

"Go ahead," Kit said, grinning. "I passed."

Nurse Yankton opened the report card and let out a low whistle. "I *mean* you passed. Almost straight As. Do you always get such good grades?"

"I usually earn Bs and Cs," Kit admitted. "No one's ever written in for tickets to see my report card. But I had plenty of time around here to study."

"Your parents should be pleased."

"I hope so. They thought I might have to go to summer school. Thank goodness I don't. I'm planning to spend every spare minute on the water. I've got to get back in shape."

"Do you have a boy friend, Kit? I mean, I don't want to pry or anything. You're such an attractive girl, I couldn't help being curious." She smiled at Kit.

"I've got several friends who are boys but nobody who is really special. Lots of guys like to fish. Lots of guys work at the marina. We're all friends."

"You got bunches of mail while you were here, Kit. Sometimes people get piles of letters and cards at first, then, after they've been here a while, they get hardly any mail at all. But there was always a letter for Kit Cummings."

"There were three other kids with me in the car the night we crashed," Kit said. "They could imagine what it was like for me being stuck here for months while they all got to return to classes. They were great pen pals. I even had a letter from the turkey who smashed into us."

"You did? What did he say?"

"Said he was sorry." Kit laughed softly. "I really felt sort of sorry for him, too. It would really be tough to know you caused someone else's pain, wouldn't it?"

"I suppose so," Nurse Yankton said. "But being sorry doesn't help much. Drunk drivers are about as bright as potholders."

"I liked his taking time to write," Kit said. "He promised not to get behind the wheel after he'd been drinking—not ever again. That's something, isn't it?"

"I suppose so." Nurse Yankton read the chart on the foot of Kit's bed. "When are your parents arriving?"

"Midafternoon." Kit glanced at the clock. One o'clock. "I just wanted to be sure to be ready. It's a three-hour drive to Key West at best; not that the overseas highway is crowded at this time of year."

"I don't blame you for being eager," the nurse said.

"I'm sort of scared," Kit admitted. "I mean I've been here for sixteen weeks. And if I'm not careful, I still limp. I don't want anyone feeling sorry for me."

"They wouldn't dare. Not if you're going to scowl at them like that."

Kit relaxed and smiled. Then she went to the mirror above the bedside table and ran a comb through her brown chin-length hair. She had cut it herself, straight and blunt and with bangs. There had been little incentive there to fool with curls, and after she got used to her new look, she really liked it. It suited her straightforward personality and the blow-and-go life style she had planned for the summer.

"What are you going to do with your Sansevieria plant?" Nurse Yankton polished a long swordlike leaf with her forefinger.

"Would you like it?" Kit asked. "It's really too large to take home in the car."

"I wasn't hinting," Nurse Yankton said. "I was just wondering. Mrs. Miller lives here in Miami, and she'll be going home soon. She might like to have it, and she might be able to take it with her when she leaves."

9

"Good idea." Kit crossed the room to the plant, examined its long waxy leaves and felt the earth around it for moisture. "I can't lift it, but maybe a maintenance person could take it to her."

"Better ask her first," Nurse Yankton suggested. "No use moving it if she doesn't want it."

Kit checked her appearance before leaving her room. Her chinos were freshly creased, and they were extra long, long enough to cover the orthopedic shoe. She wore a brown turtleneck shirt that matched her hair and a brown and tan plaid shirt over the turtleneck. The gold chain her best friend, Nita Alvarez, had sent her hung around her neck and it matched the gold studs she wore in her pierced ear lobes. She didn't care much for jewelry, but she figured that a few classic pieces might attract gazes to her head and away from her leg and foot.

"See you later," Nurse Yankton called.

"So long, Nancy," Kit said. "And thanks for everything." She left her room and walked slowly down the green hallway toward Mrs. Miller's doorway. Would she always snail pace it through life? Surely after she left this place and became more active, she would be able to move more quickly. Right now the trick was to act as if she *wanted* to walk slowly. When she reached room 115, she paused a moment, then knocked softly. Sometimes Mrs. Miller napped in the afternoon, and she didn't want to wake her if she were sleeping.

"Come in, please," a foghorn voice called.

Kit pushed the door open and entered the room. Green. Every room in the clinic was green. Mrs. Miller was almost eighty years old, but as she laughingly said, Lady Clairol kept her from looking a day over seventy-five. Now dressed in designer jeans and a shocking pink sweatshirt that fought with her red hair, she was standing at her window peering through binoculars, her trim, tall body at rigid attention.

"What do you see?" Kit asked.

"A sandpiper," Mrs. Miller said. "It's one of my favorite birds."

"They're all your favorites, aren't they?" Kit said teasingly. Mrs. Miller wrote a bird watchers' column in the *Miami Herald,* and she and Kit had spent many hours together peering through the binoculars at feathered creatures.

"I want you to meet my grandson Eric," Mrs. Miller said as she turned from the window and lowered the binoculars.

Kit looked around the room. "Where are you hiding him?" She was more eager to meet Eric than she let on. Mrs. Miller had been talking about Eric and his coming visit all week, and Kit was interested. Maybe a new friend would spice up her life.

"He'll be here after a bit," Mrs. Miller said. "I'm so glad you're going home, Kit. Eric needs to know a nice girl from Key West, a girl like you whose gears are always set for fast forward."

"Is that how I seem to you?" Kit laughed, thinking of her slowness.

"You sure do. And Eric's new in the keys, you know. Living with his older brother. He's already out of high school, so he won't have that source of new acquaintances. I know he'll be eager to meet you."

"Oh, sure," Kit said. "Granny's crippled friend from the clinic."

"Stop that, now." Mrs. Miller's piercing blue eyes flashed. "You mustn't think of yourself that way. You're well and strong. Let's see you walk for me."

Kit smiled at their ritual, their joke. She would refer to herself as a cripple, and Mrs. Miller would immediately insist that she was not and would ask to see her walk. Kit liked the reassurance in her friend's voice, and she liked to demonstrate the fact that she could walk normally. It took concentration and determination, but she could do it. Now she walked from the door to the window and back.

"Perfect," Mrs. Miller said. "It's all that whirlpool therapy that did it for you. And for me. It was magic. Pure magic."

"If you say so." Kit joked with Mrs. Miller as if they were the same age. She seldom thought of her as old. It was almost hard to believe that she had a grandson older than Kit was.

"I came to ask if you'd like to have my Sansevieria plant," Kit said.

"Oh, my dear, aren't you taking it with you?"

"There won't be room in the car. It's so tall. And there's all my scuba gear and my suitcases and three boxes of books. I'd like you to have the plant to sort of remember me by."

"I'd love to have it. You can come visit it, of course. Any time you're in Miami, you can stop by and see it."

"Thanks." Suddenly, Kit felt at a loss for words. Leaving Mrs. Miller wasn't going to be as easy as she had thought. "I'll miss you," she said tentatively.

"And I you," Mrs. Miller said. "When you see my columns in the paper, you can pretend they're letters directly to you. And you might take time to drop me a note now and then."

"I will." The promise came easy, but Kit knew the letters would come harder. She really didn't like to spend time inside writing. Before they could say anything more, someone knocked on the door.

"Yes?" Mrs. Miller called.

"Eric, gram. May I come in?"

Kit liked the voice immediately, and she was eager to see its owner.

"Do come in, Eric." Mrs. Miller walked slowly to the door, and Kit noticed that her left foot shuffled only a bit. She had suffered a stroke, and at first she hadn't been able to move her left leg or foot, but now a person could hardly tell there was a problem. She and Mrs. Miller had recovered together.

Mrs. Miller opened the door, and Kit felt her breath snag in her throat. In addition to having a magnolia and moonlight voice, the boy standing there was good-looking. He was tall and rangy, and his hair was the color of new copper as it curled crisply over his head, dangled onto his brow and tapered into carefully trimmed sideburns that stopped just below his ear lobes. Maybe he made his living posing for shampoo ads, Kit thought. At first, she couldn't tell what color his eyes were, but when he grinned, they flashed with greenish-amber lights. So this was Eric.

"Eric, I want you to meet a friend of mine, Kit Cummings from Key West. She's going home this afternoon, and I've told her that you're new in Key West. Maybe she'll introduce you to some of her friends."

13

"Hi, Kit," Eric said easily.

"Hi." Kit smelled a masculine leather scent as Eric stepped closer, and suddenly she felt as if a wedge the size of a conch shell were blocking her throat. She didn't know what to say to this boy.

"I have to go to the dispensary for some medication," Mrs. Miller said. "I want you two to sit out in our garden and watch for a green heron. Will you do that for me? I saw one out there just this morning, and I'd love to know if it's still around."

"Sure, gram. We'll green heron watch for you." Then Eric turned toward Kit. "I mean, it's fine with me if it's okay with you."

"Sure." Kit reached into her shirt pocket for her sunglasses. "It's fine with me."

"So let's go." Eric stood back to let Kit pass through the doorway first, and she walked very slowly and very carefully, knowing that she was not limping. But what a strain! She would be glad to get back to Rafe and Dave and Anita—people she could relax around. Eric made her nervous.

They walked to the end of the green hallway through the exit and into the clinic's carefully tended tropical garden. Green. But it was a natural green of philodendrons, ivies, hibiscus. And a purple Bougainvillea vine twined around the branches of an almond tree. Kit inhaled a moist earth scent and listened to the wind tease the palm fronds. She was glad when they sat on a concrete bench beneath a sea-grape tree and she tucked her feet out of sight under the bench.

"So you're from Key West," Eric said. "Gram's told me a lot about you."

"All good, no doubt," Kit said, trying unsuccessfully for a light tone. She wanted to impress the boy more than she would admit.

"Oh, definitely good. She thinks you've got a lot going for you."

Kit felt herself blushing, and she tried to change the subject. "Your grandmother is a real stitch, you know. Really laid back. She keeps everyone laughing most of the time."

"I suppose there aren't too many ladies her age who're having a love affair with designer jeans and sweatshirts."

Kit giggled. Mrs. Miller owned more pairs of jeans than Kit did, and she looked good in them, too. "What do you do in Key West, Eric?"

"Not too much right now," he replied. "My brother has a salvage business, and sometimes I work for him when he needs an extra hand. I've got my application in for several jobs, but work is hard to find this summer. What do you do?"

Kit pushed her sunglasses onto the top of her head as she often did when she needed to think. Somehow she thought the gesture helped her see the world more clearly. "I haven't been home for so long I'm not sure what I do," she admitted. "I've got to get used to being at home again before I do anything, I guess."

Eric leaned forward, propping his elbows on his knees. "I thought maybe you had a job all lined up."

"I do." She hesitated. "I mean, sort of." It wasn't a lie. She did have a job lined up.

"Give. What are you going to do?"

"My grandfather's a fishing guide. He takes fishermen out in the backwaters in his boat, the *Sea Sprite*." I'm planning to work for him this summer."

"Doing what?" Eric glanced at her with renewed interest.

"Well, gramp's eyes aren't as good as they used to be, and he has arthritis in one elbow, so sometimes I help pole the boat, and I watch for fish so I can point them out to the patrons and show them where to cast."

"What do you fish for? I mean what kind of fish?"

"Whatever kinds are available. Right now, gramp may be catching barracuda, small tarpon, permit, bonefish. We just work the shallows around the keys, the flats."

"That's the kind of fishing I'd like to know more about," Eric said.

Now Kit looked at Eric more intently, surprised to find that they really did have something in common. "Maybe you'd like to go out fishing with gramp someday."

"I have my own boat," Eric said. "A seventeen-foot fiberglass job with a flat bottom, a fishing chair and a poling platform. It's secondhand, but my brother got me a good deal on it. He thought I'd get a lot of use out of it."

"What kind of motor?"

"A hundred and fifteen horse Johnson. I call the boat the *Starfish*."

Kit tried to squelch her feelings of envy. Eric's boat sounded like the very kind of boat she had been saving her money for all her life. And she still was a long way from reaching her goal. Just when she'd think she had enough money, the boats and motors would escalate in price.

"What's the matter?" Eric asked.

"Nothing." Kit forced a smile.

"I really like to fish," Eric said. "I caught a black-tip shark just last week. He gave me a real run. My brother was along to manage the boat, and we chased that shark all over the flats."

"Did you boat him?" Kit asked, interest surmounting her prickly feelings toward Eric.

"No. He broke the line and spit the hook. I'm entered in the Key West Teen Tournament, so I'm going out after him again one of these days. I think he would have been a trophy fish. He was big. Really huge."

"So far I hold the record for black-tip shark in this year's January to July teen tournament," Kit said. "One hundred and fourteen pounds. Caught it right after the first of the year. So far no one's topped it." She wondered why she was trying so hard to impress Eric. She hated herself for bragging. But then he had been bragging, too, telling her about his superhuge shark. He had goaded her.

"Who was your witness?" Eric asked.

"My grandfather." Kit stood and felt her fingers clench into fists as she hooked her thumbs behind her belt. Was Eric implying that she had cheated? But why did she think that! Suddenly, she sensed a cold hostility between them. And she resented this new boy who had moved to her town and who was fishing in her waters and who was catching her kind of fish. She sat down again and tried to change the subject.

"Your grandmother says you're out of high school."

"Right. I am."

"Where are your parents?"

"Dad's in the army. Career man. He's stationed in Germany."

"You going there?"

"No. I'm planning to go to college next fall in Miami—if I can scrape up enough money."

"You could sell your boat." She tried not to sound happy about such a possibility, and she hated her feelings of jealousy. Being envious wasn't her style. Lots of people had boats that she would like to have, but she didn't let it bend her out of shape—not usually.

"I don't want to sell my boat," Eric said. "I may have to, but selling it will be a last resort. I'm hoping a good job will turn up."

"What do you want to study in college?" Now Kit felt a fresh surge of hostility toward Eric—Eric the scholar—and again she knew her feelings were off the wall. Her parents would like this boy—this boy who was planning to go to college. They wanted her to think about college, but so far she had refused. Negative. Who needed it? The sea had everything she wanted, and it was free. Well, it was almost free—if you owned a boat.

"I'm planning to study ancient Spanish history."

The words startled her. She had escaped into her own thoughts so deeply that she had forgotten she had asked Eric about his plans. "That sounds sort of—intellectual." She stopped herself just before she had said dull. Dullsville. That's how it sounded.

"It is intellectual, I suppose," Eric said. "That's what education's for, to stimulate the intellect. Have you ever heard of Dr. Eugene Lyon?"

"A Dr. Lyon here at the clinic?" she asked.

"No. A Ph.D. That kind of a doctor. He's a scholar who studied ancient Spanish history and was able to help Mel Fisher, the Key West treasure diver, find the wreck of an old Spanish galleon that had tons of priceless artifacts aboard."

"Everyone in the keys has heard of Fisher," Kit said. "But I never heard of Dr. Lyon."

Eric sighed and grinned. "I suppose scholars aren't as glamorous as treasure divers."

"And I don't think they have as much fun as fishermen."

"Maybe. Maybe not. Who's to say? Are you going to enter the new fishing tournament in July?"

"Sure thing." She did plan to enter. She didn't know if her leg would be strong enough for such strenuous sport, but she didn't tell Eric that. "The new tournament won't start for two weeks, so first I'm going to win a trophy in the current tournament." She heard her voice grow harsh and high, but she couldn't make herself shut up. "I plan to win the black-tip trophy. I know the flats. I've fished them with my grandfather ever since I was old enough to go out in a boat. I'm going to top my own record during these next two weeks."

"Hey, mellow out." Eric looked surprised at her tirade; then he squinted his left eye as he spoke. "I don't know the flats, but I've got my own boat, and I do know how to throw a lure so a shark can't resist it. I'm going to give you some strong competition for that trophy, Kit Cummings, and two weeks will give me plenty of time."

Eric rose and strode back into the clinic, leaving

her alone. Why had she bragged so? Was she trying to compensate for being laid up for four months? She was mad at herself, *ashamed* of herself. Mrs. Miller had been her friend for all those long weeks, and the first thing she had done was to antagonize her grandson. Why couldn't she have been nice!

2

Kit returned to her room and made arrangements for an orderly to move the Sansevieria plant to Mrs. Miller's room. Mrs. Miller had gone with a nurse to a therapy session by the time Kit's parents arrived, and Kit left her a note, promising to write to her later.

Back in her own room, Kit smelled lilac perfume an instant before her mother appeared in her doorway.

"Kit!" Her mother rushed to her, hugged her, her blue eyes brimming with unshed tears of happiness. "It's good to see you. We can hardly wait to have you back home again."

"And I can hardly wait to be home, mom! It's been a long pull." She eyed her mother, tall, slim, her heart-shaped face lightly tanned, her brown hair a bit sun bleached. And, as usual, she wore a blue

21

outfit. That day it was a slim-skirted travel suit. People said she and her mother looked alike, and Kit always enjoyed that comment. She could do a lot worse than to look like her mother.

"Where's dad?" Kit glanced toward the door, suddenly uneasy. "You didn't drive up here alone, did you?"

"Of course not." Her mother looked around the hospital room and began gathering up Kit's things. "Your dad's outside parking the car. I just came on ahead to see if you were ready to leave."

As Mrs. Cummings spoke, her husband entered the room, bringing with him the faint odor of paint that frequently clung to him since he had begun restoring their old Conch house. That day, although he wore dress slacks and a fresh sport shirt, the I've-been-working-with-paint aroma was still notice-able. And the room suddenly seemed smaller. Big boned, barrel chested, tall, her dad seemed to absorb space.

"Kitten!" His brown eyes twinkled as he wrapped her in a bear hug. "Ready to shake loose from this place?"

"You bet I am, dad. I can't wait."

"Then let's go," her mother said. "Are you checked out?"

"Yes. The doctors and nurses took care of all the details this morning. All we have to do is to carry my things to the car and sign out at the front desk."

"I'll carry the scuba gear," her dad said. "Mary, can you take the suitcase?"

Her mother picked up the suitcase. Kit felt useless at not being able to help, but when she picked up a small box of books, her father shook his head and took it from her.

"You and your mother go on to the car, Kit, and I'll come back for the rest of the things. The doctor said you were to avoid overexertion."

"Carrying a small carton of books is hardly over-exerting." Kit laughed, wondering how she was going to break from the role of invalid without hurting her parents' feelings.

The car trunk yawned like an open mouth, and her father dumped the scuba gear into it, added the suitcase her mother had carried, then returned to her room for another load. Mrs. Cummings opened the rear door for Kit, tried ineffectively to help her inside, then took her own place in the front passenger seat.

"Are you sure you're comfortable, dear?" Her blue eyes clouded with concern.

"I'm fine, mom. Really I am."

"It's going to be a long ride. I hope you're up to it."

"I'm dying for it to start," Kit said. "Does Nita know I'm coming in today?"

"Yes. She's called to check with me every day since she got your letter."

Kit could hardly wait to see her friends again, and once her dad returned with the last of her things, she looked toward the sea as they headed south, easing through the traffic, nosing on toward the keys.

Kit always imagined that the overseas highway was a shining necklace and that the keys were emerald sets in that necklace that stretched between

Miami and Key West. That day it was as if she wore a special antenna that picked up sensory details she had almost forgotten: the sweet briny smell of the Gulf Stream, the taste of salt in the soft trade wind wafting through the car window, the hum of the car tires against concrete, the screeching of a gull. Everywhere she looked, she saw the endless sea whitecapped with foam, sequined with multicolored sailboats. And here and there men in fishing boats pulled in red and white buoys and checked their lobster traps. Home. The Cummings Conch house sat on Fleming Street, but the sea was her true home.

After two hours of travel, they stopped at Marathon for a sandwich; when they were in the car again, Kit knew they would be home within the hour. Big Pine Key, Sugarloaf Key. Then Stock Island. In a few more minutes, they turned onto Roosevelt Boulevard and headed toward the Old Town district of Key West. Fleming Street.

"How does gramp like living in the condo?" Kit asked. "Does he miss us and the house?"

"I think he's adjusting very well," her mother said. "Climbing those steep steps to the second floor was getting to be too much for him. I think he thoroughly enjoys the condo with its elevator."

Kit craned her neck to see all the houses they passed. Many Cuban families lived in that part of town, and many of them rented rooms for tourists during the winter season. People from up north liked to explore the old Conch houses. Over a century before, during the heyday of the sailing ships, Key West had become the salvage capital of the world. At that time, Kit's great-great-grandfather had moved the Cummings home to Key West from the Bahamas. Kit felt that her home was very special, and she didn't mind if tourists looked at it. But most of the tourists were gone now.

"What are you doing to the place?" Kit asked as she eyed three sawhorses on the second-floor gallery that ringed the white frame house.

"I started by giving it a new coat of paint," her father said. "You know how the salt air down here laps up paint as if it were ice cream. I'm planning to repair the pine walls on the second floor before the summer ends, and I need to replace some stair treads. I've noticed, too, that some of the fancy gingerbread work on the porch needs retouching."

When the car stopped, Kit was the first one out, and she stood for a moment just staring at the house, which gleamed like a birthday cake in its new coat of white paint. She had to lean her head far back to see the widow's walk atop the steeply slanted roof, and her mother took her arm, guiding her around one of the cables that lashed the frame of the house to the ground, giving the structure extra endurance when hurricane gales whipped the island.

"It's beautiful, dad. Just beautiful! Makes every other house on the block look drab by comparison."

"Flattery will get you everywhere," her dad said.

"Let's go to the kitchen for a glass of limeade before we unpack," her mother suggested.

Kit knew the suggestion was a ploy to delay her climb to the second floor, but she was willing to take time to stretch her legs, to refresh herself with a cool drink. Once inside the house, she headed straight for the kitchen, but on the way, she noted the familiar surroundings, the pine-paneled walls, the pine ceil-

25

ings. Her dad was proud of the house because his great-grandfather had built it using no nails, only pegs and dovetail joints. The house had been knocked apart in Nassau years earlier and loaded aboard a sailing ship for the voyage to Key West. Sometimes at night, when the trade wind was wafting into the attic's ceiling scuppers, Kit tried to imagine her great-great-grandfather pacing on the widow's walk, peering at the sea through a telescope, searching for ships in distress. For that had been his business—salvaging wrecks from the reef that surrounded the island.

They had hardly seated themselves in the cool blue and white kitchen when the telephone rang, and Mrs. Cummings hurried to answer it. For Kit, the blue of the curtains and the tablecloth was a welcome change from the green of the clinic. It was cool. Restful. It was good to be home.

"The phone's for you, Kit." Her mother handed her the receiver after pulling the phone on its long extension cord to the table. "Nita."

"Hi, Nita," Kit said eagerly. "What's up?"

"Thought you'd never get here," Nita's husky voice drawled. "How about a tour of the island? I can pick you up in five secs."

"Hey, I'm not even unpacked yet," Kit said. "Can you wait an hour or so? We just now arrived."

"Sure, Kit. See you in an hour. Seems like you've been gone forever."

"Yeah, it does at that. See you, Nita."

After she replaced the receiver, she noticed her father's worried look. "I don't know, Kit. The doctor said you weren't to overdo."

"I'm just going for a ride with Nita," Kit said. "That hardly comes under the heading of overdoing, dad. Really it doesn't."

"She's right, Jim," her mother said. "The doctor also said we weren't to coddle her. He said she was to ease back into her regular life style as long as she didn't overtire herself."

"Cars." Her dad spat the word. "I hate to see you get in a car, Kit. I know it's unreasonable, but—"

"Dad, be realistic. I can't spend the rest of my life avoiding cars. Nita's a careful driver. The accident wasn't her fault. It was the fault of that drunk driver."

"The world is full of drunk drivers, Kit. The laws—"

"Let's drink our limeades and forget about drunk drivers," her mother said, bringing out cookies to go along with their drinks.

"Gee but it's great to be home," Kit said at last. "You can't imagine how much I missed you, missed everyone. I can hardly wait to see gramp."

"He had a charter today, but I think he'll stop by tonight to say hello."

After they finished their limeades, Mr. Cummings carried Kit's suitcase to her room, then stored the scuba gear in the garage. Her mother climbed the stairs to her room with her, and they stood for a few moments on the second-story porch.

"I thought the climb might be too much for you," her mother said.

"It was a piece of cake." Kit tried to hide the fact that she was almost panting from the exertion. Her great-great-grandfather had saved indoor space by building the stairway to the second floor on the outside of the house; consequently, it took more steps to reach her room than it would have had the stairway been inside. She wished she could climb the tiny companionway to the attic and mount the ladder to the widow's walk, but that was out of the question until she regained more strength.

Her mother helped her unpack, opening her suitcase on the butter-yellow bedspread that matched the curtains and the throw rugs. All the yellow, along with the natural pine walls, gave her room a sunny look even on a cloudy day. Kit loved her room, loved the seascape on the south wall and the cork board on the west wall that held citations from dozens of fishing tournaments. Usually, Kit released her catch, and that action had won her many good sportsmanship awards.

"Does gramp have a charter for tomorrow?" Kit asked.

"I don't know what his plans for tomorrow are, Kit."

"If he does, I want to go along."

"Do you really think you're up to that?" Again, her mother's eyes clouded with concern. "I mean there's no point in rushing into a situation that may be too much for you. Let's take things gradually."

"Okay, mom. Don't worry about it. I won't bite off more than I can chew."

By the time the unpacking was finished and the suitcase stored away, Nita had pulled her VW up to the curb and was alighting. Kit started to run down the stairs to meet her, then stopped, suddenly realizing she couldn't run—at least not safely. She waved to Nita from the upper porch, then walked down the steps and out to meet her.

"Hey, no limp!" Nita called out in her outspoken manner. "That's great."

"I told you I didn't plan to limp through the rest of my life." Kit laughed, more relieved than she cared to admit, now that this first encounter was over. Nita hadn't changed. She was as bouncy and bubbly as ever, and she still wore her black hair in a wedge cut brushed back from her face. Her dark eyes danced with an inner glee, and as usual her mouth was open. She often joked that she had been born with one gene programed for constant chatter and that a girl could hardly be expected to talk with her mouth closed.

"Tell me all about it, Kit. What did you do in that hospital for four months? Four months! An eternity. Thought you'd never get home."

Kit opened her mouth to reply, but Nita didn't give her the chance. "Hey, I've got big news. Big news! But I'll save it until after we pick up Dave and Rafe."

"We're picking up the boys?"

"Yeah! They're dying to see you, too, you know. It'll be like old times. We'll scoop the loop and maybe stop for a burger somewhere."

"I can't stay out too long," Kit said. "My gramp is coming over, and dad doesn't want me to overdo on this first day home."

"Sure. Sure." Nita drove along Front Street past the alley that led to Mallory dock, turned left on Duval Street, then stopped on a corner in front of a bookstore where David and Rafe stood waiting.

They hopped into the back seat, trying to greet Kit, close doors and seat themselves all at the same time.

"Good to see you, Kit," David said. "Really super."

"Yeah!" Rafe agreed. "Thought you'd never get back."

Kit smiled at her two friends. Blond, blue-eyed David Rollins was so big and muscular he had to hunch his shoulders to squeeze into the VW. He was a football player, totally devoted to athletics in the fall and to Nita the rest of the year. Rafe Mira was slightly built, and his olive skin was so sun bronzed he looked like a pen and ink sketch in his white shirt and jeans. Kit had dated Rafe some, but mostly they were just good friends.

After the initial comments, a silence fell over the car, and nobody could seem to think of anything to say to break the awkward quiet. At last, Kit remembered about Nita's big news. "Nita, what were you going to tell us? You know, you said you had news."

"Right." Nita drove slowly past Smathers Beach, which was almost deserted. Kit watched the last rays of sunshine glinting on the red brick of West Martello Gallery, the old Civil War fortress; then Nita spoke again. "I'm going up north for the summer."

"Nita! You can't do that!" Kit looked at Nita for an in-depth explanation. "I mean I just got home, and now you're leaving!"

"Right. But I'll be back in the fall. I'm just going up to Marathon to work as a receptionist in a condo sales office for the summer. It's a great job. Neat salary. Lots of fringe benefits. It'll prove life after debt."

Kit tried to be glad for Nita's sake, but she wondered who she was going to talk to during the summer. She and Nita had been very close. In fact, Nita was her only close girl friend. The rest of her friends were boys, and while she liked them, she couldn't talk with them about personal things the way she could with Nita.

"What are you doing this summer, Rafe?" Kit asked, thinking that while Rafe talked, she could sort of get used to Nita's surprise announcement.

"I'm still waiting tables at Casa Marina in the coffee shop. Breakfast and lunch. Then I'm still doing my juggling act on the dock in the evenings."

"How are the crowds?" Kit asked.

"Fair. But they're appreciative. They give when I send the hat around."

Now they had passed the airport and East Martello Gallery and were driving along Roosevelt Boulevard approaching McDonald's. Kit smelled the aroma of hot grease.

"Anyone for a burger?" David asked. "I'll treat."

"Can't pass up an offer like that." Nita signaled a left turn, and they rolled into the drive-in just as an old Ford jalopy wheeled out. The driver of the Ford waved, and Kit was surprised to recognize Eric. Even in the twilight, his coppery hair gave him a living-color aura that made the rest of the world seem like a black and white backdrop. So he had a car *and* a boat! Some deal. Again, she felt herself bristling toward him. Why couldn't she forget about him! She hadn't actually promised Mrs. Miller she'd take Eric under her wing.

"Hey, who's that?" Nita asked. "I've never seen him around before. He looks sorta neat."

31

"He's just a guy I met at the clinic. His name's Eric Miller. His grandmother and I were friends."

"He looked at you as if he'd like to trade on that friendship," David said.

"Wonder where he hangs out," Rafe said. "You know, Kit?"

Surprised, she realized she didn't know. She hadn't asked Eric where he lived. And now she wondered. Did he live in Old Town? She doubted it. He seemed more like the kind who'd be at home in the fancy Flagler Avenue neighborhood. But she was only guessing. She knew a lot about Eric's boat and his fishing plans but little about anything else concerning him. "He's new to me, gang. Just met him for a few minutes this afternoon."

They ate burgers and fries while they watched the sun sink into the bay. Kit thought they really should have been at Mallory. That's where everyone went to watch the sunset. Then, suddenly, she realized that Rafe had taken time off from his juggling act just to greet her on her first night home, and she felt rather special. A gull wheeled overhead, waiting for a scrap, and she tossed a crust of bread. Swooping, the gull caught the crust in midair and flapped toward the bay.

"The beggars," David said. "We spoil them with our handouts. If they ever had to fend for themselves, they'd probably starve."

"I wouldn't grieve over it," Rafe said. "There'll always be someone around with a crust. It goes with the territory."

It was good to see her friends again, but Kit was tired and ready to go home by the time Nita headed in that direction. Nita let the boys out first; then, when she pulled up at the curb in front of Kit's house, she sighed.

"I'm leaving at six in the morning, Kit."

"We hardly got to see each other!" Kit protested.

"Maybe you can drive up to Marathon sometime," Nita said. "It's not all that far, you know."

"Yeah, maybe." Kit knew she would be unlikely to drive to Marathon. She planned to spend every spare moment fishing. "I'm glad you came over tonight, Nita. It's so good to see you and the guys again. But what am I going to do without you all summer!"

Nita revved the motor as if she didn't know what else to say. "Wish I hadn't taken the job now, Kit. Really I do. But it's too late to back out."

"I wouldn't want you to miss out on a job on my account," Kit said. "You know that."

"Yeah, I know." Nita revved the motor again.

Kit got out of the car, feeling awkward and ill at ease and sad all at the same time. "See ya, Nita." She stood on the sidewalk watching as Nita drove away. Then, when the car was out of sight, she went inside. She couldn't believe she could feel so let down. What if she hadn't come home that day? She wouldn't have seen Nita at all! She looked at her mother and blurted out her feelings.

"Mom, Nita's spending the summer in Marathon! She's leaving tomorrow."

"I know," Mrs. Cummings said.

"But why didn't you tell me? I mean, how am I going to get along without her? First the rehab clinic and now this. It isn't fair."

"Maybe it's for the best, Kit."

"Mom! How can you say a thing like that. Nita

and I have been friends since kindergarten. I need her."

"Maybe you need her just a bit too much, Kit. Maybe a little more separation will give both you girls a chance to grow on your own, to develop your own thoughts and opinions."

"Mom!"

"I know it's hard to think about another separation right now, but the summer will go quickly. You'll see."

Kit changed the subject quickly before she and her mother got into a real argument. She didn't need that on her first day home. "Gramp stopped by yet?"

"He's been here and gone," her mother said. "He's sorry he missed you, but he couldn't stay. He had a rough day, and he does have a charter tomorrow."

"I could drive over to see him," Kit suggested.

Her father shook his head. "Not tonight, Kit. Dad's very tired. Maybe tomorrow you can mo-ped to the marina, see him before he goes out for the day."

"Good deal!" Kit felt guilty at not being home when gramp stopped by, but she would make it up to him. She would get up early and see him at the marina. If he didn't have a helper, maybe she could go out with him for the day. She wished she had talked to him. She didn't know whether or not he had hired someone to help him.

Kit watched a little TV with her parents, trying all the while to forget about Nita's departure and the fact that she had missed seeing her grandfather on her first night home. She went to bed early. A warm bath eased the twinges in her leg, and she fell asleep almost before her head touched the pillow.

The next morning, she awakened without aid of an alarm, and she was up and dressed and downstairs before her parents made an appearance. Her mother arrived first, dressed in a trim suit and ready for her day at the library, and a few minutes later her dad appeared, wearing paint-spattered jeans and a T-shirt that hugged his muscular shoulders.

They ate a quick breakfast; then Kit spoke. "Mom, if I drive you to the library, may I take the car to the marina? I'm not sure I'm up to riding my mo-ped just yet."

"You may take the car without driving me to work, Kit. I've been walking lately. It's just a few blocks, and I need the exercise."

"Hey, neat!" Kit helped herself to another piece of toast. "I may go out with gramp today if he'll have me. Wow! Do you realize how long it's been since I've gone fishing?"

"Too long," her father replied. "But if you go out today, you be careful. Don't overdo. You're going to need some time to get your strength back in that leg."

"I'll be careful, dad. Don't worry about it." Kit gulped the rest of her breakfast, grabbed the car keys and walked to the car. Thank goodness it was her left leg that was weak. She had no problem driving the few miles to Stock Island and Sea Haven Marina where gramp kept the *Sea Sprite*.

She breathed in the salt-scented air as she parked in a visitor's slot and hurried toward the pine dock that stretched into the calm water of the bight. Here the stench of diesel fuel hung in the air, and the forklift on a tractor squeaked a protest as it lowered a small boat from its dry berth high in a covered shed. On the dock, fishing-boat captains called greetings to each other as they lined up at the pumps to take on fuel.

Kit shaded her eyes with her hand, looking for her grandfather. And suddenly she realized she was looking for Eric, too. He had to keep his boat somewhere. But she didn't see him, and at last she did see her grandfather's sea-blue boat and his stooped figure in the stern, clad in its usual sea-blue jump suit. She walked toward him, smiling. Gramp was stocky and of medium build, but he looked sturdy as a dock piling and like a man at ease with himself and his world.

"Gramp! Hi! Sorry I missed you last night."

Her grandfather, peering from beneath the visor of his sea-blue cap, his weather-creased face wreathed in a smile, turned to greet her. "Kit! Good to see you. You look sound as a dollar."

"Is that good or bad?" Kit asked with a laugh, thinking that gramp's tough, steel-mesh voice hadn't changed since she last heard it.

"It's good. The saying holds true in spite of the economy." Gramp paused in wiping the dew from the gunwale of his boat. "You got time for a cup of coffee?"

"Have *you* got time?" Kit asked. "That's more to the point. All I've got is time. You have a firm charter for today?"

"Yes, but he's not due to show for half an hour

yet, and I'm all ready to go." He dropped the damp cloth onto the bottom of the boat, stepped over the gunwale and joined Kit on the dock. "Come on. Let's have some coffee—hot chocolate for you, if you prefer that."

"Good deal, gramp. We need to talk." Kit walked ahead of her grandfather into the nearby tackle shop, taking care not to limp, and they sat down at a small coffee bar at one end of the shop.

"One coffee black and one hot chocolate," gramp said to the waitress. Then he turned to Kit. "Glad to be home?"

"That's an understatement, gramp. I'm wild to be home! Who you taking out today?"

"A fellow from Iowa. Wants to catch a permit."

"They been hitting lately?"

Gramp shrugged. "You know how it is. Sometimes yes. Sometimes no. I think I know a spot where we might see a few if we're lucky."

"Gramp?"

He looked at her, waiting.

"May I go out with you? I mean, how have you been managing while I've been away?"

"Look here, girl. Don't talk to me like I'm over the hill. I've got a lot of good years left in me yet."

"Of course you have, gramp. But you know what I mean. I want to go out with you. I can hardly wait to get my hands on that pole again. Where are we going today? Toward the Marquesas? Farther on toward Dry Tortugas? That's where you find permit, isn't it?"

Her grandfather sat silently for so long that she stopped sipping her chocolate and looked directly at him. "Gramp, you are going to take me out with you, aren't you? I mean, it's what I've been waiting for, for four long months."

Her grandfather looked at his coffee cup and shook his head. "I can't do it, Kit. No way. Try to understand. I just can't do it."

"Tell me you're joking." Kit felt her stomach muscles knot, and she pushed her sunglasses to the top of her head. "Gramp, what do you mean?"

"No. That's what I mean. No. I've talked this over with your dad, Kit. He's told me what the doctor had to say about that leg of yours. You need to rest it, to work it gradually. You don't need to be taking chances with it, not the kind of chances you'd be taking on that poling platform. I've got to say no. It's for your own good."

"I've rested my leg for four months, gramp." Kit shoved her cocoa aside. "I've got to get back on the water. Can't you understand that? We'll work together. It wouldn't be as if I had to work the whole day from the platform. We can take turns. I'll pole when your shoulder hurts. You can pole when my leg needs a rest. We'll make a team."

Gramp shook his head. "No way, Kit. No way. I'm as eager as you are to see you back enjoying your normal activities again, but I don't want to be responsible for you. I know you. You're so gung ho for fishing that your leg could fall off and you wouldn't notice unless it caused you to lose a fish. You just rest up this summer. Maybe come fall we'll go out. Let's not rush it."

"Come fall. *Come fall!* You know I'll have to be back in school then, gramp." Then, suddenly, Kit grew quiet. She knew her grandfather almost better than he knew himself. He was stubborn. If he said no, he meant no, and no amount of wheedling on her part would change his decision. She slid from the stool, ignored her unfinished hot chocolate and left the shop. Tears blurred her vision as she stepped onto the dock and walked back to the family car. She waited until her vision cleared before she started driving home.

Gramp had deserted her. Gramp, the one person she thought she could trust and depend on, had deserted her. She couldn't even imagine what she was going to do with her summer without gramp and the *Sea Sprite* and without Nita. She might as well be back in Miami in the clinic! Why was everyone babying her so? The doctor hadn't said she had to give up everything and humor her leg. He hadn't said that at all. He had merely said to use good judgment. Why was everyone turning against her? How was she ever going to save money for a boat if she had no job?

3

Kit returned home to an empty house. A note on the kitchen table advised her that her father was at the paint store, and of course she knew her mother would be at the library all day. Her mood matched the blue kitchen, but she knew tears wouldn't help. As her thinking became more rational, she realized that her grandfather was only doing what he thought was best for her. She couldn't hold that against him. But it griped her to think that everyone thought they knew what was best for her. Nobody paid any attention to what she thought was best.

Sunshine slanting through yellow curtains cheered her as she hurried to her room, and it was a few moments before she realized she actually was *hurrying*. And her leg felt fine. She walked with even greater confidence. So what if she limped a bit. It was great to know she could get up a little speed when she needed it.

She walked to her desk, found paper, pen, thumbtacks. Then she sat down to think, to write out some trial words for the signs she intended to make. GUIDE FOR HIRE. K. L. CUMMINGS. Five years' experience. Knows the backwaters. Your boat. Your tackle. Phone 762-8546. $100 full day. $50.00 half day.

She played with the words, rearranging them this way and that until she achieved the effect she wanted. Then she hand printed three signs. Returning to the car, she drove to the marina again and posted one sign on the bulletin board in the security office, another in the marina office and the third at the tackle shop near the dock. The signs might do no good, but at least they made her feel as if she were taking action on her own behalf. If she intended to be a professional fishing guide, there was no time like the present to get started.

Once she reached home again, her dad was at work, painting the garage. "Want some help?" Kit asked.

"Thanks, but no." He smiled at her. "Just have one decent brush. You might stick around to talk to me, though. We've got some catching up to do."

Kit sat on a bench at the redwood picnic table, which was shaded by an almond tree. She would be able to hear the telephone if it rang. No use sitting in the house on such a nice day. She looked at the banana tree, the sea grapes and the palms, but they did little to lift her from her glum mood.

"I suppose you know gramp refused to let me fish with him today," she said.

"I guessed as much." Her dad dipped his brush into the paint can, then applied it to the garage siding. "Try to understand, Kit."

"I understand. I'll just have to prove to him that I'm really no invalid. I had counted on working for gramp this summer, dad. I need the bucks. If I'm ever going to save enough money to buy my own boat and motor, I need to work. And without work I'll die of terminal boredom."

Her father cleared his throat. "Have you thought any more about going to college, Kit? You've some money saved. And your mother and I'll help you all we can. A college education would be like an insurance policy. You could fall back on it if the charter business wasn't all you dreamed it would be."

Kit pushed her sunglasses onto the top of her head and looked directly at her dad. "I don't need a college education to take people fishing." Kit kept her tone light. They had covered that ground all too often. "All I need is a boat and a motor. I know more about the flats and the backwaters around here than most of the professional guides. Gramp will vouch for that."

"I know you know the territory," her dad said. "But what seems to be a great idea for a career at age seventeen or eighteen may seem less appropriate as you grow older. The time to get your education is while you're young."

"I'll think about it, dad." That was the phrase she always used to shut off the college talk. "What would you like for lunch?"

"Is it lunch time already?"

"Almost. What would you like? I'll make it, and we can eat out here on the picnic table."

"How about avocado salad? Lots of lettuce and tomato and a whole avocado."

"Sounds great." Kit went inside to see if everything she needed was in the refrigerator. All the time she was making their salads, she was listening for the telephone. But it remained silent. What had she expected? Anyone planning to fish that day would have set up their trip for early morning. But maybe someone would call about fishing the next day.

She and her father ate lunch; then she went to her room to rest and read during the heat of the day. It was almost five o'clock when the telephone finally rang. She answered it on the first ring.

"Hello. Kit speaking."

"This is Maggie at the marina, Kit. Got a job for you tomorrow. A Captain Hartley would like to go out in the morning for a half day and perhaps a whole day, depending on the luck you have during the half day."

"Hey, great! What time does he want to leave?"

"Eight o'clock sharp. He'll bring the lunch."

"Good deal. I'll be there." She hesitated a moment. "Maggie?"

"Yeah?"

"What's he like?"

"Young. Polite. Neat looking."

"Did you see his boat?"

"No, but he said it was in good condition and that he'd have it here ready to go."

"Good. I'll see you in the morning."

"Good luck, Kit. Hope he's congenial."

"Me, too. See ya, Maggie."

Kit was so excited she could hardly keep from spilling her secret to her parents. But she kept quiet. They might forbid her to go out in the morning if they knew. She wasn't too keen about going out alone with a stranger in a strange boat, but that was part of the business. She could handle it. She would require him to register at the marina office. That was a safeguard.

After helping her mother prepare red snapper and coleslaw for dinner that night, Kit enjoyed her meal, then retired for the night. Nobody questioned her decision of an early bedtime. They seemed to expect it. Early the next morning, she dressed in jeans, a blue and white gingham shirt and a billed cap. It felt good to get back into her fishing clothes. She rode her mo-ped to Stock Island, parking it near the marina office. It pleased her to know she had the strength to ride it. The day before, she had doubted it. It was a step forward. Dew glistened on the palms near the office door, and the humid air carried the living-fish scent of the sea. Once inside the office, she blinked, letting her eyes adjust to the dimness.

"Captain Hartley?" she asked Maggie. "Has he shown up yet?"

"He's on the dock at pump number two taking on fuel, Kit. A very young captain and really good-looking. Wouldn't mind spending the day with him myself."

"Hope he's as nice as he looks." Kit grinned at Maggie and headed toward the gas pumps. Before she reached the second pump, she stopped. Captain Hartley's back was to her, but she would have recognized his shampoo-ad hair anywhere. That morning, the sun highlighted pink glints in the copper-colored curls that matched his knit shirt. Before Kit could speak, he turned.

"Hello." He spoke coolly, ramming his hands into the pockets of his faded jeans. "You going fishing today, too?"

"I have a charter for today." Kit admired the sleek lines of the *Starfish*. "Maggie in the office said Captain Hartley was waiting for me at pump number two. She must have been mistaken."

Eric's left eye squinted, and he pressed his lips into a flat line. "Who's kidding who around here? I'm Captain Hartley, and I'm expecting a guide named K. L. Cummings."

"Katherine Lee Cummings at your service." Kit swallowed around a faint catching of her breath as she gave Eric a mock salute. "At least I used my real name."

"And so did I," Eric said.

"Oh, pardon me. I guess I just imagined that your name was Eric Miller."

"I guess you did at that." His left eye squinted even more, and his lips didn't relax. "My grandmother's name is Miller, but she's my mother's mother. My name is Hartley. And I was expecting a *man* to guide me for the morning."

"Want to cancel out?" Kit couldn't keep the taunting tone from her voice. A boat captain who failed to keep his end of a bargain would have a hard time finding another guide willing to work with him.

Eric sighed and forced a smile. "No. I don't want to cancel. A deal's a deal. I want to go out, and I want to catch a tarpon."

"Thought you were hot for black-tip."

"I want to try for tarpon first," Eric said. "I've never caught one of those."

"Sorry," Kit said. "I make no promises as to the kind of fish you'll catch or even *if* you'll catch, but I can assure you that I'll take you where the fish are."

"And you know where the tarpon are?" Eric asked.

"Yes."

"Yes? That's all there is to it? You know?"

"That's right. I know. But unless you know how to deal with tarpon, you may only catch 'cuda."

"I know what I'm doing. Let's go to your tarpon spot. And don't think I'm going to waste my time on 'cuda."

"Have you ever caught 'cuda on the flats?" Kit asked.

"No."

"That's what I thought. 'Cuda aren't much fun in deep water, but they can deal you a real battle on the flats. Don't knock 'cuda fishing in thin water until you've tried it."

"Who runs the boat?" Eric asked, maneuvering them through the bottle-green water and heading away from the dock.

"You can take the wheel and I'll show you where to go, or I'll take the wheel. Choose what you feel most comfortable with." Kit studied the small cream-colored boat as she eased into the stern. "You got plenty of tackle?"

"You take the wheel," Eric offered. "And yes, I've plenty of tackle. I've brought those foot-long pink tube lures for black-tip and also some squid if you want to use fresh bait."

"The tube lure will be okay for tarpon, too." Kit took the wheel, while Eric sat ahead of her on the fishing chair. She opened the motor once they were away from the marina, heading north. The bow slammed into the waves with resounding cracks, and she slowed down a little as she saw Eric holding on to keep from being thrown from his seat. Turning his head toward her, he shouted above the roar of the motor. "Where are we going?"

"I know a special channel up this way where tarpon hide out the year around. You may be lucky enough to get a hit." She raced on toward the channel, tasting the salt spray that misted against her lips, watching the sun reflect rainbow hues in the V-shaped froth of water at the bow. Several minutes later, she slowed the *Starfish* again as they approached the fishing grounds.

"This it?" Eric pulled a cream-colored fishing cap from a bulkhead compartment and jammed it onto his head.

"This is it." Kit cut the motor and pulled the pole from the gunwale clamps. "I'll pole while you fish from the bow. The tide's coming in fast, and it's a prime time for tarpon, shark, 'cuda. Get ready. Everything's happening at this tide stage."

Kit eyed knee-deep water so clear it might have been ginger ale. Wide strands of green-gray turtle grass streamed just beneath the surface, following the motion of the waves. Here and there, white sandy patches humped through the grass.

"Cast toward those sandy spots," Kit advised.

"Tube lure?" Eric asked.

She nodded. "Cast and let the lure sink. Then

47

work it slowly." She paused, easing her weight onto her right leg as she tried to rest her left leg. The wind and the current were strong, and it took all her effort to keep the boat moving along slowly in the desired direction.

"There!" she called softly. "See that swirl?"

"Where?" Eric asked, never taking his eyes from the water.

"Two o'clock. Throw, man, throw."

Eric looked to his right to where the number two would be on a clock face, then made the cast and let the lure sink.

"Hold your rod tip low and crank the reel slowly," Kit advised. "Maybe flip the lure just a little. Tarpon are lazy fish. They want the lure right at their nose."

Eric reeled in his line and threw again.

"If you get a hit, it'll feel like you've picked up weed at first. That's the time to set your hook. Sometimes tarpon strike, then do a fast spit and get away. You've got to act quickly at the right time."

Eric reeled the line in again, and Kit turned the boat so he would have the advantage of the wind with his next cast. No good. The bait tube hooked onto itself, forming a pink doughnut, and he had to reel it in and straighten it out. The next cast was a good one, and seconds after it hit the surface, a fish struck.

"I think it's a 'cuda," Kit yelled. "Reel! Crank! Keep your rod in front of you."

But the advice came too late. Eric let the rod get behind him, and from that position, he had no more room left in which to maneuver it.

"He's off." Kit sighed, trying not to sound irritated. "You've got to keep that rod in front of you

48

where you have plenty of room to maneuver it." As she spoke, they heard a loud splash.

"What was that?" Eric asked.

"Tarpon. Sometimes they do a slow, lazy roll as they gulp air. They make a sharper sound when they're feeding. You'll soon learn the difference once you've heard both sounds a few times."

"Where'd you learn all so much about fishing?" Eric asked.

"I told you. From my grandfather. I've been going out with him for years. Where have you fished that you don't know more about the backwaters?"

"Up north. Canada. Up there I like to fish for muskies."

"Some of the same techniques apply." Kit said. "Gramp says that a muskie fisherman is usually a good tarpon fisherman. Hang in there and keep trying. Want to try a plastic worm instead of the tube?"

"Will it work?"

"Sometimes. It's worth a try."

Eric changed lures and continued casting. He threw dozens of times; then he stopped and rubbed his right arm. Kit knew his arm was aching. Her leg was aching, too, but she kept on poling. She wanted to place any responsibility for slowing down on Eric rather than on herself.

"If your arm's worn out, we can rest awhile," she suggested.

"Can't catch anything with the lure in the boat," Eric said.

"Right. But you can't catch anything with a tired arm, either. Better rest before exhaustion sets in."

"Then how about lunch?" Eric asked.

Kit glanced at her watch, then at the tide chart she carried in her pocket. "Let's make a quick run to a new spot, okay? I'd like to get there before the tide changes too much. Don't want to get us stuck on a sandbar. The running time will give your arm a rest."

"Where's the new spot?" Eric asked.

"A ways back south toward the Marquesas," Kit replied. "I know some secret places around there where the tarpon hang out."

"Let's go for it, then." Eric sat down, jammed his visored cap more tightly onto his head and faced into the wind. "By the way, what's that white blimp up in the sky?" He pointed. "It never seems to move?"

"Oh, that's Fat Albert." Kit laughed. "It's a blimp full of surveillance equipment that keeps track of what's going on in Cuba. There's a cable lashing it to the ground."

"Wow! You mean if Castro is getting ready to attack, Fat Albert will be the first to know?"

"I hope so." Kit stopped laughing. "Guess I never thought much about it before." She fitted the pole in the gunwale clamps, switched on the motor and pointed the bow into a deep-water channel that they followed until they passed Stock Island and Key West, until the Marquesas islands came into view. Presently, she cut the motor and let the boat drift onto the flats where the water was clear but very shallow. A white egret waded in the sea to their right, and a cormorant sunned himself on a coral rock directly ahead of them.

Then Eric reached into his ice storage compartment beneath the poling platform and pulled out two Saran-wrapped submarine sandwiches and two cans of Coke. He handed one of each to Kit and kept the rest.

"My favorite!" Kit unwrapped her sandwich and began eating.

"Hey, look!" Eric stood and pointed. "There goes a ray. A big fellow! Really humongous!"

"Good deal, Eric. Where a guy sees rays, he's also likely to see 'cuda, bones, black-tip." She began gulping her sandwich, washing it down with huge swallows of Coke. And even before she was finished eating, she saw a black-tipped fin break the surface.

"Look. One o'clock. See it? Shark!"

"How big?" Eric stood on the bow, peering at the sea as he shaded his eyes with his hand.

"Couldn't tell, but it looked big enough to be of interest. Want to try for it?"

"Sure." Eric laid his half-eaten sandwich on the boat seat, then pulled a slip powerhead from a portside compartment and loaded it. Then he picked up his rod and attached a pink tube lure.

Kit felt a pain stab up her left leg as she took her place on the poling platform once again. Maybe she should speak up. Maybe she should insist on going in. Eric had only hired her for a half day, and by the time they reached the marina, it would be far past noon. She was just about to verbalize her decision when Eric yelled.

"There he is! Right there! Three o'clock!"

Kit looked to her right and saw a sluggish gray-green body gliding through the water, parting the turtle grass as it moved.

51

"Stand on the bow," she called to Eric. "You can see better from up there. And drop that lure right in front of his nose."

"That close?"

"Right. A shark has poor vision. You need to plunk the lure right in front of him. But don't hit him with it. You've got to be superaccurate with your cast. You hit him, you'll scare him up to Miami."

Kit had lost the shark's location, but she kept her gaze on the water; presently, she saw the sleek green body drifting toward them. Seconds later, a black-tipped fin cut through the surface again. She pointed. "See it?"

"He's coming this way."

"Throw!" Kit's mouth was so dry she could hardly speak. Something about hooking a black-tip was more exciting than hooking other kinds of fish. That's the way it was for her, anyway. She didn't know how Eric felt about it.

Eric's aim was near perfect. The lure splashed just ahead of the shark's nose. He caught it, and the rod tip began to bend toward the water. In the next instant, the shark streaked toward the horizon.

"You've hooked him," Kit shouted. "He's on!"

In the distance, the shark jumped, and the line peeled from the reel. Kit forgot about the pain in her leg as she climbed from the poling platform and started the motor. They followed the shark across the shallows. When the *Starfish* drew close to it, Kit gasped. It was hard to judge weight when a fish was still in the water, but she guessed this one to be close to 130 pounds. Or maybe even bigger.

"How big do black-tip get?" Eric asked.

"Maybe a hundred and fifty pounds. Maybe more."

"And how big was the one you caught? The one that holds the record?"

"Keep your mind on your fish," Kit snapped. "You haven't boated him yet."

For the next forty-five minutes, they followed the shark in its zigzag course across the flats. Eric's head and face streamed with sweat, and his shoulders sagged in a way that revealed his exhaustion.

"You want to bring it aboard?" Kit asked.

"Of course I want to bring it aboard." Eric's left eye squinted. "You crazy or something?"

"You'll have to kill it to bring it aboard," Kit pointed out. "I thought you might want to release it. There are sportsmanship awards for—"

"Is there any way to weigh it without bringing it aboard?" he asked.

Kit shook her head. "No."

"You know how to use a powerhead?"

"Yes. Where is it?" She knew where it was. She had only asked to delay having to use it.

"It's in the bulkhead compartment. Portside." Eric ground the words between clenched teeth. "It's loaded and ready to go."

Kit found the powerhead, lifted it carefully from the compartment, then eased toward the bow with it, trying to hide her distaste for that part of the fishing scene. The shark was tiring, and Eric had reeled it right to the side of the boat.

"There he is," Eric said. "A real monster. Can you get him?"

"Yes." Reluctantly, Kit dropped to her knees,

leaned over the gunwale and took aim. But the minute she pulled the trigger on the powerhead, she knew something was wrong. The thing had misfired, and the shark was unharmed but filled with a fear that gave it new life. Now it streaked toward the horizon again, startling Eric so that he almost lost his grip on the rod. As he fumbled to gain control again, the shark threw the hook and disappeared from sight.

Neither Kit nor Eric spoke for a few moments. They just stood staring in the direction of the shark's disappearance. At last, Kit found her voice.

"Rough deal, Eric. That was a nice one. Too bad."

"Too bad? Too bad!" Eric's left eye narrowed as he shouted the words. "That really tears it! You let that shark get away. You misfired the powerhead on purpose."

Kit looked at Eric to see if he was joking, but she knew immediately that he wasn't. His show of unfair anger dismayed her. Up until then, she had enjoyed the morning in spite of the initial misunderstanding. She had begun to change her mind about Eric, to think he was really okay. His husky, soft voice had fascinated her. His looks had attracted her, too— that gleaming hair, those broad shoulders, his strong hands. But, in an instant, all that faded, and her own anger was a red mist blinding her to everything else.

4

Kit fought to keep her cool. "I most certainly didn't let the shark get away on purpose. How can you say such a thing?"

"Who holds the local record for black-tip?"

"I do."

"At what weight?"

"One hundred and fourteen pounds."

"And that fish would have weighed at least one-thirty. You didn't want me to bring him in, did you? You didn't want me to ruin your record. Kit Cummings, you're a cheater. You're a common cheat. There's nothing wrong with the powerhead. You deliberately caused it to misfire."

Anger paralyzed Kit's vocal cords. She hooked her thumbs behind her belt and clenched her fingers. She would have left Eric and walked back to Key West if she could have. But that was impossible. Nor could she merely turn the boat over to Eric in strange waters. She corked her pride, switched on the motor and sped them back to the marina. By then her leg was aching so badly she could hardly hold back the tears. She had learned two things that day. She had learned that she hated Eric Hartley and that she wasn't yet strong enough to work as a fishing guide.

When they reached the marina, she handed Eric the key to his boat, stepped onto the dock and enjoyed the supreme satisfaction of refusing the fifty dollars he offered her for her morning's work.

Anger still bubbled deep inside her when she reached home, anger at Eric for his unfair accusation that she intentionally let the shark escape, anger at herself for pushing herself to impossible physical limits. Thank goodness both her parents were out! She knew she couldn't bear talking about what had happened. Neither her mother nor her father were the kind to say, "I told you so," but she knew they would be thinking those words if they learned that her leg was aching.

Grabbing the aspirin bottle, she gulped two tablets with some cold milk, then limped upstairs and ran hot water into the tub. She had soaked for a half hour before her leg felt better. But it did feel better. That was the important thing. As she stepped from the tub and grabbed a towel, she could still hear Dr. Crawford's voice giving advice and instructions.

"Your leg will tell you what you can and can't do. Listen to it. If you have pain, ease up. Don't overexert. As long as you feel comfortable, you'll know you're doing okay. Strength in that leg will return gradually if you're patient."

Patient! How could she be patient when she was watching her whole future swirling right down the tubes! Lots of the girls in her class wanted to be secretaries or lawyers or engineers or artists or musicians. Most of them wanted jobs that would keep them indoors. Kit thought she couldn't bear a life of being cooped up inside four walls. That's why she thought that operating a backwater charter boat was such a perfect thing for her. She would be outdoors all day long. She would be doing the thing she loved most—fishing. And she would be earning a good living at it. How could things have gone so wrong! Even her sunshine-yellow room failed to revive her spirits as she dressed in chinos and a tank top and went downstairs.

"Kit?" her mother called as she returned from work. "You home?"

"In here, mom." Kit poked her head through the kitchen doorway, then stepped back to the table and finished setting out dishes for their supper.

Her mother strolled to the kitchen doorway, pulling off her gold earrings, untying the belt on her blue shirtwaist and kicking from her high-heeled sandals. "Did you have a good day on the flats?"

Kit thought of sugar-coating the truth, then decided against it. "Had a rotten day. A really rotten day."

Her mother cocked her head the way she usually did when she was puzzled or worried. "What happened? Who did you go out with?"

"I went out with Mrs. Miller's grandson. You know the lady at the clinic that I told you about? His name's Eric Hartley, and he has his own boat."

"And he hired you to guide for him?"

"Right. He doesn't know the area, so he wanted a guide who did."

"And what went wrong?"

Kit decided to omit the tale about the shark. "My leg went wrong. It started aching before noon. I was lucky Eric had signed up for only a half day."

"Why don't you sit down and rest, Kit? I can set the table and get the supper on. You rest."

"I'm okay now, mom. I gave the old leg a hot soak, took a couple of aspirins. It's feeling a lot better now. But I know I'll never be able to work a full day on the flats. At least not for a while."

"Nor should you try to, Kit."

"But I need the money."

"There are other ways to earn money. Maybe I could get you on as a page at the library."

"It would bug me to be indoors all day, mom. I'd really hate it."

"What's all this hate about?" Her dad came through the back doorway, wiping the perspiration from his forehead on his shirt-sleeve, filling the room with his presence.

Kit repeated her story quickly. "Mom offered to try to get a job at the library, but working indoors would really be a ho-hummer."

"Say!" her dad exclaimed. "That reminds me. Rafe Mira called here this morning wanting you, Kit. Said he'd call this evening before six. And he said something about a job."

"Wonder what that could be." Kit glanced at the wall clock.

"He also said something about asking for a favor," her dad said. "I didn't press for details."

Kit mixed a salad while her mother made conch

58

fritters, and they sat down to an early supper. The family enjoyed eating early because it left a longer evening for reading or other activities. During supper, Mr. Cummings told of a summer job he had waiting for him once he finished the major work on their house and garage.

"Managing the snack bar on a day-trip fishing boat?" Kit asked. "Do you really think you'll like that sort of thing?"

"I don't know, but a job's better than no job, and I don't intend to sit around all summer just waiting for school to start again."

Just then, the telephone rang, and Mr. Cummings answered. He turned toward Kit. "For you. Eric Hartley."

Kit felt an angry flush rise from her neck and cover her face. "Tell him I'm out, dad. Please. I don't want to talk to him."

Her dad hesitated; then he made polite excuses and replaced the receiver. "What's with you and Eric Hartley?" he asked.

"Nothing. I just don't want to talk to him."

Kit felt guilty at refusing the call, but she tried to put it from her mind. She didn't need Eric Hartley. She said no more about jobs, but she was deeply concerned about the summer. No Nita. No fishing. And no library job—she hoped. After they finished eating, she helped straighten the kitchen. She had all but forgotten about Rafe Mira until he knocked at the door.

"Thought he was going to call," she whispered to her dad.

"Maybe he meant call in person, Kit. Answer the door."

Kit smiled at Rafe through the screen. "Come on in, Rafe. Dad said you telephoned." She eyed Rafe's juggler's outfit—tight red pants, pink tank top that showed off his tan, red ballet-type shoes. And he carried a red over-the-shoulder satchel that she knew contained his juggling pins and balls.

"I can't stay but a second," Rafe said. "But I've got a deal for you."

"What sort of a deal?" She motioned Rafe to the couch, and he sat, perching uneasily on the edge of the cushion.

"It's sort of a job offer," Rafe said. "And if you take it, I'll benefit from it, too."

"Explain. Give." Kit smiled, wondering what he had in mind.

"Well, since I'm only working at the Casa Marina during the mornings, I have most of my afternoons and evenings free. I signed on with a company called Lower Keys Enterprises to help them advertise their new condominium on Big Pine Key. If I sign up some more advertising helpers, I'll get a commission. You could do it, Kit. I mean if you need a job, it would be a start for you until you find something better."

"I don't know." Kit shoved her blunt-cut hair behind her ears. "Tell me more about it."

"It's an easy thing." Rafe opened his satchel and pulled out some advertising flyers. "All you have to do is to pass these flyers out to people on the street. I pass mine out over at Mallory dock before and after my act. There's always a crowd there at this time of evening."

"And Lower Keys Enterprises pays you for passing out the flyers? How do they know you really pass them out?"

Rafe pointed to his signature at the bottom of one of the flyers. "You have to sign the flyers. Then you pass them out. When anyone shows up at the condo and presents one of the advertising sheets with your name on it, they get twenty-five dollars for their trouble, and the company sends you twenty-five dollars because your name's on the sheet."

"Oh." Kit thought about the advertising arrangement. "How much have you made at this?"

"Fifty dollars so far," Rafe said. "And I just started this week. If you agree to work, I'll get an extra buck or two for every flyer that shows up with your name on it because I recruited you as a worker."

"I don't know," Kit said.

"How about coming with me to the dock tonight?" Rafe looked at his watch. "I've still got time to set up my act. Then, after I finish performing, I'll pass out flyers. You can see how it goes."

"Okay, Rafe. I'd like to see your act. I haven't been to the dock in ages." Kit told her parents she was leaving, and she and Rafe walked toward his brown Honda, which was parked at the curb.

"We could walk to the dock if it's okay to leave my car here."

Kit thought of her leg, of the exercise she had already had that day. "I'd rather ride, Rafe. Okay?"

A flush reddened Rafe's tanned face. "Oh, sure, Kit. I forgot about the leg. Sorry."

Kit smiled broadly. "Don't be sorry, Rafe. That's one of the best compliments I've had lately. I'm dying for everyone to forget about my leg. It's just that I think I'd better ride this evening."

Rafe drove to Front Street, then entered the alley leading to the dock. They had no trouble finding a parking place. The summer crowd of spectators was small compared to the throngs that showed up during the winter tourist season.

"What's that droning sound?" Kit asked.

"You'll see soon enough." Rafe grinned. "You've got to see it to believe it."

"Where do you set up for your act?"

"Think I'll try the far end of the dock tonight. Plenty of room there. And it's quieter."

Kit smelled the fragrance of banana bread wafting from a vendor's cart. "Looks as if there are some new acts. At least they're new to me." Then she spotted the source of the droning and moved away from it. "Look at the guy with the bagpipes! I've never seen him around before."

"He came about a month ago." Rafe laughed. "He has this end of the dock pretty much to himself."

"There's a new magician," Kit said.

"Yeah. He shows up about every other night. Guess you've seen the tightrope walker, haven't you?"

Kit nodded. "He was here before I left. And so was the singing group with the blond-haired girl who plays the saw." Kit sat on the cement wall at the edge of the dock, positioning herself so she could watch the sinking sun as well as Rafe's juggling act. A turbaned woman on a large red tricycle rode through the crowd chanting, "Key West lime—Key

West prime. Cool and refreshing. Get your Key West limeade now. Key West lime—Key West prime . . ."

Kit shook her head as the woman glanced in her direction, then rode on. Now Rafe was holding three orange balls in his left hand as he blew a blast on a conch shell he held in his right hand. At the loud wailing sound, people turned to look and listen. Rafe continued sounding the conch until a small group of people gathered around him. Then he placed the shell back in his satchel and began tossing the orange balls, giving a line of chatter as he expertly caught the balls without missing. As more of a crowd gathered, he set a red felt hat on the cement at his feet.

"Feed the kitty if you like my act, folks. Feed the kitty." Rafe juggled five balls at a time, doing fancy throws between his legs, letting one ball roll slowly around his neck as he bent his head to accommodate it. Then, as a finale, he performed a fire-baton act, keeping six flaming batons in action at the same time.

A round of applause filled the air when he concluded his act, and many people dropped bills and coins into the hat before they strolled on to watch another act in progress.

"What did you think?" Rafe asked, approaching Kit after he had packed away his things.

"You've improved, Rafe. I've never seen the flaming-baton number before."

"It's new." He smiled his pleasure. "I'm still perfecting it, but the crowd doesn't know that."

"How much did you take in tonight?"

"Eighteen bucks and some change. Not too bad."

"Want me to help you pass out your flyers?" Kit asked.

"No sense in passing out ones with my name. I'll give you some I haven't signed yet, and you can sign them. Might as well promote your own name. Might as well get started. I can sign you up on the official worker's blank tomorrow. Nobody's going to rush up the road to view the condo tonight."

"Okay," Kit agreed. "I suppose it won't hurt anything for me to give it a try."

Rafe gave Kit a stack of the flyers along with a ballpoint. "Have at it, Kit. The more you hand out, the more chances you have of making some bucks."

Kit took the flyers and sat back down on the concrete wall to sign them. But she couldn't keep her mind on the writing. All around her, people were talking and laughing, and as she looked across the sea, she could count fourteen sailboats skimming across the deep green water of the bay to dock for the night. She smiled to herself. Her dad used to have a sailboat, and he used to take her and her mother out for an hour or so before sunset. Then he would try to bring them in just as the sun was sinking. Kit had pretended that they were movie stars and that the tourists on the dock were taking their picture for some important Hollywood film rather than for their personal photo albums that would record their Key West vacation.

"Red sails in the sunset." Her mother used to sing those words to a poignant melody as they floated past the dock. But they didn't have the boat any longer. They had sold it and applied the money toward a new fishing boat for gramp, a boat that had some conveniences that made it easier for him to operate it in spite of his stiff joints.

"Hey, that's the way!" a man shouted from the crowd. "Let's hear it for Mother Nature!" The man began to applaud as the sun disappeared into the sea.

"Atta girl, M. N.," another voice called. And the spattering of applause rose, then ebbed quickly.

"Guess that show's over for another night," Rafe said, joining Kit. "How you doing with the signatures?"

"Got a dozen or so done." Kit grinned. "I got to watching the sunset and sort of forgot about business."

"Sign a few more, and then let's go over to those steps. You can hand them to people as they leave the dock. Hurry it up or you'll miss out on the crowd. People don't hang around long after they've applauded the sunset."

Kit scrawled her name on ten more flyers; then she stood, getting ready to walk to the steps and to the crowd. But before she could leave the dock's edge, a boat caught her eye, a cream-colored boat with Eric Hartley at the wheel. His back was to her, but she recognized both Eric and the *Starfish*. She would have looked away instantly if it hadn't been for the girl facing Eric as she sat on the bow of the boat.

"Someone you know?" Rafe asked. "Isn't that the guy we saw at McDonald's?"

"Yes," Kit answered. "His name's Eric Hartley, not Eric Miller. I took him out fishing today. We had a really rotten time."

"Hey, girl, you don't have to explain to me, you

know. It was just an idle question. Who's the chick with him?"

"Don't know who she is, Rafe." Kit looked at the girl more closely, glad that Eric's back was toward her. Tall. Slim. She had long thick hair, the pale shimmery color of white wine, and she had pale skin that looked as if it had never seen the sun. The girl had a misty appearance, like a blurred photograph that makes the observer squint and take a careful second look. But why was she so interested in Eric Hartley's girl? He certainly meant nothing to her, and his grandmother certainly didn't need to worry about his finding friends in Key West! Clearly, Eric was not the sort to have troubles of that kind.

"Come on, Kit." Rafe pulled gently on her wrist, urging her to the steps. "Come on before all the crowd leaves. It's hard to pass out flyers when there aren't any people left to pass them out to. Move it."

Kit smiled up into Rafe's face just as Eric turned the *Starfish* and came in close alongside the dock. Kit stared down at him, wondering if he was going to hit a dock piling, then looked away quickly when she was sure he was safe.

"Kit?" he called to her. "Kit?"

Kit turned her back and pretended not to hear. She had nothing more to say to Eric Hartley.

"Hey," Rafe said, "that dude's calling to you, Kit."

"You must be mistaken, Rafe. I didn't hear a thing." She linked her arm through Rafe's and urged him toward the crowd at the dock steps.

5

Rafe drove Kit home, leaving a stack of condominium flyers with her, and promised to telephone her name to the company first thing the next morning. The formal registration blank could be mailed later.

"Thanks, Rafe," Kit said as they parted. "I appreciate having a job of sorts. Maybe if I really give it my best shot, I can make it pay off."

"I suppose a lot of the success of it depends on pure luck," Rafe admitted. "A guy knows that most people are just going to pitch those flyers in the nearest trash can. But some people do go take a tour of the condos. The twenty-five bucks they get is enough to pay for their gasoline and lunch. Some people make a day's outing of it."

"I hope so," Kit said. "Thanks again, Rafe. Maybe it'll work out for both of us." She waved good-bye and walked into the house. After explaining to her parents the details of Rafe's job offer, she sat at the living room desk and began signing more flyers.

"We're going out for an ice cream cone," her dad said. "Want to come along?"

"No, thanks, dad." Kit sighed. "It'll take me all night to sign my name on this stack of sheets."

"Okay, Kitten. We'll see you a little later."

At first, signing the flyers was fun. She tried for effect, signing her name in different ways, huge capitals and tiny lower-case letters, back-slanted writing, a signature that sloped upward on the page. Then she settled down to writing her normal signature. Is this how famous actresses who signed lots of autographs felt? Bored with the whole thing? She paused to flex her cramped fingers.

Eric Hartley. Eric Hartley. His name zinged through her thoughts, and she felt ashamed. She couldn't remember ever having refused a phone call or ever having turned her back, refusing to speak to a person who had spoken to her first. Never. Why had she been such a nerd? Anger, of course. She was still smarting from Eric's unfair accusation concerning the shark. But he hadn't seemed angry that night. That was strange. She stopped signing flyers as she thought about it, and she tried to recall the expression on his face. It hadn't been exactly a happy expression, but his face definitely had not been filled with anger. His left eye hadn't been squinted, and his lips hadn't been pressed into that thin white line that showed his displeasure.

She wondered about the pale-haired girl with him. Who was she? Pretty in a misty sort of way. She was the kind of girl a person would notice and remember, but Kit couldn't recall having seen her before. She glanced at the telephone. Maybe she should call Eric and apologize for snubbing him. Her reaction had been totally uncalled for. Snubbing people wasn't her sort of thing. What if Eric told his grandmother? She flushed at the thought. Mrs. Miller had gone out of her way to be kind to her at the clinic. The only favor she had ever asked in return was that Kit help Eric meet some friends in Key West.

"He won't be in the book," she said half aloud as she shoved the condo flyers aside and walked to the telephone. She looked in the thin directory just to be sure. She was right. There were no Hartleys listed. She dialed a number for information.

"What city please?" the operator asked.

"Key West."

"Name, please?"

"Eric Hartley?"

There was a long silence; then the operator spoke again. "I have no Eric Hartley listed. Do you know where he lives."

"No, I don't," Kit said. "I do know that he lives with his brother here in Key West."

"I have a Henry Hartley listed. I can give you that number."

"Fine." Kit jotted the number on the corner of the telephone directory, then replaced the receiver. Did she really want to dial the number? She really didn't want to call, but she knew she had to. She had to try to set things right between herself and Eric for Mrs. Miller's sake if for no other reason.

Kit smiled ruefully, knowing she was kidding herself. She wanted to call Eric because in spite of all her negative feelings about him, she was attracted to him in some crazy sort of way. She liked his looks. She liked his boat. She liked the way he had handled himself on the thin water of the flats. She guessed that Eric liked fishing almost as much as she did. But enough introspection. As she dialed the Henry Hartley number, she wished she had asked the operator the street address. She would like to know where Eric lived.

The line hummed and crackled for an instant; then she heard the busy signal buzzing in her ear. She listened to it for a second or two before she replaced the receiver. Busy line. Who could Eric be calling. Or maybe his brother was on the line. Maybe Eric was still out with Miss Misty. Maybe they were going to make a night of it. Maybe right this minute they were at Sloppy Joe's or Captain Tony's. Just because Rafe had brought her right home from the dock was no reason to think that Eric would have taken his date home so early. She sighed, dialed the phone number again and waited. Another busy signal.

So much for calling Eric. She replaced the receiver and returned to the desk and the stack of condo flyers. She signed twenty more of the ads, and as she paused again to rest her fingers, someone knocked at the door. Shoving her chair away from the desk, she rose and went to answer the knock, snapping on the porch light before she opened the door.

"Oh, hello!" Again, her breath snagged in her throat. She was surprised to see Eric standing on the porch shifting his weight from one foot to the other and looking totally uncomfortable as the overhead light glinted on his coppery hair. "Want to come in?" She held the screen open and stood aside so he could enter.

"I've just stopped by for a minute . . . to apologize." Eric blurted the last two words as if they hurt his tongue and he was eager to spit them out. Kit saw a slow flush rise from his neck, giving a rosy hue to the bronze tan of his skin.

"That's a coincidence," she said. "I just tried to telephone you . . . to apologize." She felt uneasy being so near him.

Eric smiled tentatively. "You have nothing to apologize for, Kit. Nothing at all."

"It's not my habit to refuse phone calls or to snub people at the dock, Eric. I heard you speak to me, and you know it. I was still angry about this morning, and I just wasn't going to give you the satisfaction of a reply. I'm sorry. And I really did try to telephone you just a few minutes ago." She hoped he believed her.

"I don't blame you for cutting me dead." Eric looked at his left shoe. "Kit, I examined that powerhead after I docked my boat. It was faulty. A spring had worked loose. There was no way you could have fired the thing correctly. No way at all."

"Are you sure?"

"I'm positive. That shark was destined to be a free fish."

"I'm relieved." Kit smiled broadly at Eric.

"Relieved? You're glad it got away." Eric's left eye narrowed into a squint.

"No. I don't mean that. It's just that in the back of my mind I had begun to doubt myself—my own motivations. I do hold the black-tip record, and I do want to be high-point person in that category again this year. I got to worrying that maybe, subconsciously, I had deliberately misfired the powerhead. I mean, you were so angry and . . . and . . . I just began to doubt myself."

"Truce?" Eric grinned at her.

"Truce." She smiled back at him.

"Want to celebrate the armistice over a soda?" he asked. "We could stop by the Lime Tree. I don't have a car tonight, but we could walk."

"You mean you walked over here?"

"Sure. It's not all that far. I just live on Simonton Street. How about it? Want to walk to the Lime Tree?"

Kit hesitated. She really did want to go to the Lime Tree with Eric, but she didn't feel up to walking the distance. And she didn't want to embarrass him or herself by saying so. A fleeting thought chased through her mind. What had he done with his girl friend? But that was his problem, not hers.

"Why don't we stay here, Eric? I'll make us sundaes, and we can sit on the patio."

"Fine with me, if that's what you'd rather do."

"You can help me. Come on." Kit led the way into the kitchen, got two blue dishes from the cupboard and took the ice-cream carton from the freezer. "Want to dip?" she asked. "Two scoops in each dish; then I'll add the topping. You like chocolate syrup or kumquat jam?"

Eric began dipping the ice cream. "I'll go for the kumquat. Never tried that before."

"We have a kumquat tree in the back yard. It's really almost a nuisance. Keeps someone busy raking up the fruit. And according to mom, jam is about the only thing they're good for."

Kit added the topping to the ice cream, picked up two blue napkins, two spoons, and carried everything out the back door and onto the patio. They sat at the redwood table under the almond tree, and the rising moon bathed the whole yard in a silvery glow.

"Smell the jasmine?" Kit took a deep breath.

"Smells good," Eric replied.

"Never could understand how a flower that's a real zero in the daytime can smell so good after dark." She picked a jasmine blossom and laid it on the table between them.

"This is some neat spot," Eric said as he spooned up a bite of his sundae. "Tell me about some of these trees. I recognize the palms and the banana, but what's the one to our left?"

"Avocado. And the ones near the hedge are sea grape. Where are you from, Eric? I know your grandmother said 'up north,' but where?"

"Indiana. My parents were divorced, and I lived with my father. But he got an overseas assignment a couple months ago, so I decided to come here and live with my brother. Since I'm planning to go to college in the fall, Henry decided I should spend some time down here where it all happened."

"Where what all happened?"

"I told you I'm planning to major in ancient Spanish history. Key West was on the sea route of the Spanish treasure galleons that used to sail between Old Spain and the New World. I think this is a very exciting place."

"Depends on what your thing is, I guess," Kit

said. "I think Key West is a very exciting place when I'm out on the flats fishing. I've never thought much about Spanish galleons or sunken treasure, but I do know that Mel Fisher has an exhibition set up in that old brick building near Mallory dock."

"Don't think I haven't seen it! I practically lived there the first few days I was here. All those gold chains. All those pieces of eight. You've seen the exhibition, haven't you?"

"Oh, sure. I saw it when he had it aboard a replica galleon docked near Caroline Street."

"A replica galleon! Hey, I'd really like to see that."

"Too late. It sank."

"Did he lose a lot of the treasure?"

"I don't think so. They brought up everything that was of value."

"My brother has worked for Fisher," Eric said. "Not steadily, but part-time now and then when his own business slacked off."

"He's in the salvage business? Isn't that what you told me?"

"Right. He has his own boat. Anyone loses anything in the sea, Henry can help them retrieve it."

"Are you going to work for your brother this summer?"

"I don't know yet. I may have to."

"*Have to?* I think it sounds rather interesting. Do you dive?"

"Yes. I've got my license."

Before Eric could say more, a sharp splashing sound drew their attention to a reflecting pool beneath the sea-grape trees.

"What was that?" Eric asked.

"Come look." Kit stood and started toward the pool. "But wait a sec." She went into the house, then returned with a crust of bread.

Eric joined her at the edge of the pool where lava rock ringed the silver-black water. Kit dropped a few crumbs of bread into the pool, and in seconds there was a swirling of the water; then a golden body broke the surface, and the crumbs disappeared.

"What was that?"

"My pet goldfish." Kit laughed. "Really. That's what it was."

"But it was a foot long! Easily a foot long."

"I got the goldfish as a birthday gift a few years ago when they were about two inches long. I kept them in a bowl in my room for a long time. Then I got tired of taking care of them and changing the water and all."

"Yeah," Eric said. "I know how it goes. I used to have a pet turtle."

"Mom said I should get rid of the fish if I wasn't going to care for them properly, but I hated to give them away. So dad came to my rescue. He converted this old cistern into a reflecting pool, and we put the goldfish in it. They grew."

"That's the understatement of the year!" Eric laughed and tossed another crumb into the water. "How deep is the pool?"

"About ten feet, I think. Years ago, when my great-grandparents lived here, the cistern was their source of drinking water. There was no fresh water piped from the mainland as there is today. Every house had a steeply slanted roof like the one on our house, and a series of downspouts carried rain water to the cistern."

"That's really neat," Eric said. "Remind me never to fall into your pool. A giant goldfish might swallow me!"

Kit laughed, surprised at how easy it was to talk to Eric. She considered asking about the girl in the boat with him, but she couldn't bring herself to do it. Talking to him wasn't *that* easy. She didn't want to press her luck.

They returned to the redwood table and watched moonlight filtering through the broad almond leaves, listened to the trade wind murmur through the leaves on the banana tree.

"Would you like more ice cream?" Kit asked.

"No, thanks. It was really good, but I've had enough."

They sat in a silence that was comfortable at first, but it grew rather strained after a few minutes. Kit could think of nothing more to say. She wished her parents would come home. Her dad was a talker. He could start a conversation with anyone, and he knew how to keep it going.

"Would you like a Coke?" she asked at last.

"No thanks, Kit. If you'd like one, go ahead."

"No, I don't want one, either."

Again, silence. Was Eric feeling as ill at ease as she was? Maybe he wanted to go home and didn't know how to make the break. But surely not. A tree frog chirped in the sea grape, and another frog answered from their neighbor's yard.

"Kit, I have an idea," Eric said at last. "But I don't know what you'll think of it."

"Lay it on me and we'll see what I think of it." She felt a pulse point in her throat begin throbbing. What was he about to suggest? A date?

"You speak of loving to fish, yet you have no boat, right?"

"Right. But I'm saving my money to buy one."

"That doesn't help you much right now, does it?"

"Hardly at all. I usually help my grandfather on the *Sea Sprite,* but he's hired someone else for the summer."

"How did that happen? Didn't he know you were being released from the clinic?"

"He knew." Kit tried to keep her tone light, but it was hard to do. "Gramp's afraid I'll overdo and strain my injured leg. He doesn't want to be the cause of my downfall."

"That's tough. Sometimes it's impossible to reason with the people who care the most about you, isn't it?"

Kit looked at Eric, pleased that he seemed to understand her feelings. "You're right. It is. But how did you know?"

"In a way, I have the same problem. I've known forever that I want to study ancient Spanish history. But dad wants me to consider joining the army. He's a career man, you see. I guess he wants to see one of his sons follow in his footsteps, and Henry's made it clear that he isn't going to be the one to do it."

"So that leaves you, right?"

"Sort of. I mean dad won't force me to join up, but neither will he help me financially with college. If I enroll, I'll have to pay my own way."

"That's tough. It'll take big bucks, won't it?"

"Right. But I don't intend to let money or the lack of it stop me. I don't intend to spend my life doing jobs that bore me. I'm willing to work for what I want."

"Work for your brother?"

"If I work for Henry, I'll have to lay out of school for a year before I'll have enough money to pay my tuition. But I have another idea that could help both of us."

"Both of us?" Kit looked at Eric in surprise, but in the soft moon glow, she couldn't interpret his expression.

"We both need money; me for college, you for your own boat, right?"

"Right."

"And neither of us can make much working for someone else, agreed?"

Kit thought of the condo flyers inside on the desk and the scant chance that a few people would pick up on the offer to visit the condo for a tour when they knew a salesman would be giving them the hard sell before they left the grounds.

"Right again, Eric. But what are you leading up to?"

"Maybe we could form a partnership for the summer, Kit. A *business* partnership. I've got a boat that's suitable for fishing the flats. I'm eighteen, and I've got a license that allows me to carry paying passengers in that boat. The thing I don't have is an in-depth knowledge of the fishing area—the flats, the channels, the changing tides."

Kit began to smile. "And while I have no boat or commercial license, I know the flats like I know my own bathtub. I know the channels. I know where certain kinds of fish like to feed. I know the kind of baits and lures they go for."

"Right," Eric said. "Between the two of us, we

have what it takes to run a profitable charter business. The going rate for a boat and a guide is right at two hundred dollars a day. We could split the take fifty-fifty and come up with a hundred dollars each. If we went out seven days a week we'd make seven hundred dollars a week. We'd almost—"

"Hold it! Hold it, Eric. The idea sounds good in theory, but summer isn't the peak fishing season in the keys, you know. Gramp has worked these flats all his life, and I don't think he's *ever* had a charter for every day of the month. If he goes out three times a week during the summer season, he's doing well. And there are expenses involved, too. Gasoline. Motor maintenance. Marina fees."

Eric paused thoughtfully. "We could split expenses, too. Taking customers fishing would still be better than any salaried job we could find."

"Right," Kit agreed. "It would. I just didn't want you to see it as a piece of cake."

"What do you think? Would you be willing to give it a try?"

"I'd need to think about it. I'd need to talk it over with my folks and see what they think. I'm sure they'd want to meet you before they made any suggestions."

Eric looked toward the driveway where a car was just turning in. "Looks as if they might have that opportunity right now. Do you want to introduce me to them, or do you want me to come back another time?"

"I'll introduce you right now. I want you to meet them whether or not we work out a business deal."

Kit waited until her parents got out of the car;

then she called to them. A business deal. She had to remember that all Eric had suggested was a business deal, a plan for them to earn some money during the summer. As she smiled up at her parents, she remembered the blond-haired girl who had been in Eric's boat less than two hours earlier.

6

After Kit performed the introductions, her parents joined her and Eric on the bricked patio, pulling up yard chairs near the banana tree and the palm.

"Eric has an idea for us to work together this summer," Kit said. "We'd be taking people backwater fishing in his boat, with me serving as guide. We'd like your opinion on the plan. Do you think it would work for us?"

"But your leg," her mother blurted. Then she apologized. "I'm sorry, Kit. I hate to keep reminding you of it, but—"

"I'm sorry, too," Eric said. "I forgot about your injuries. Maybe this isn't a good idea."

"But I think it will work," Kit insisted. "I can operate the *Starfish* and serve as guide, deciding when and where we'll fish. When we reach the flats, you can mount the platform and pole the boat across the water. That's the strenuous part of a day's trip, the poling. If the wind and currents are against you, it takes a lot of muscle to move even a small boat like yours."

"Your boat's seaworthy?" Mr. Cummings asked.

"Yes, sir. I bought it through my brother. Henry's in the salvage business, and he knows the importance of having a sound boat and dependable motors. The *Starfish* is in good shape. You're welcome to check it out if you care to."

"I checked it out this morning," Kit said, smiling. "It's a neat craft, dad."

"You have ship-to-shore radio?" her mother asked.

"Yes, ma'am. Henry installed it for me, and we've tested it. You see, I was planning to try guiding on my own. I have a license. It wasn't until I went out with Kit this morning that I realized how much there is to learn about the flats and the channels and the tides. I'd hate to take someone fishing and get trapped on a sandbar with no way off until the next high tide."

Mr. Cummings laughed. "That can happen, Eric. I'm glad you're aware of that danger. Even seasoned guides sometimes get caught, much to their embarrassment."

"They see a fish or maybe a school of fish, and they want to give their customer one more chance at them," Kit explained. "Gramp got caught that way once a couple of years ago."

"What did he do?" Eric asked.

"He saw his mistake in time to take action. He got out of the boat, made his customer get out, too, and together they waded, pulling the *Sea Sprite* by a bowline until they reached deeper water. It was very embarrassing for gramp."

"What about tackle, Eric?" Mr. Cummings asked. "You have to be prepared with lots of rods and line and lures. You'll be taking out people who have never fished before and who know nothing about casting techniques. You'll lose a lot of tackle."

"Some people bring their own tackle," Kit said.

"But most don't," her father added. "You'll need to provide an ample supply."

"I'll talk to Henry about it," Eric said. "I have quite a bit of good tackle, but he'll be able to put me in touch with people who can help me assemble some more. I've built a few rods of my own from kits."

"We'll share expenses as well as profits," Kit said.

"If you've taken all these things into consideration, then I see no reason why you can't try guiding," Mr. Cummings said. "You may have a hard time finding a marina that will let you work from its dock. Summer is a slack fishing season. The marinas may have all the guides they need."

"I hadn't considered that," Eric admitted. "I thought maybe we could just work from a public dock."

"People usually go to a marina to inquire about guides and charter boats," Mr. Cummings said. "You usually have to be affiliated with a marina if you hope to get any business."

Eric faced Kit. "Looks as if the first thing we need to do is to go marina hunting. Are you free in the morning?"

Kit hesitated, remembering Rafe and the flyers on

83

her desk. She would have to explain to Rafe. Maybe she could help him find someone else to distribute the ads.

"I mean if you're busy in the morning, we could wait until afternoon," Eric said. "But we need to find a marina as soon as we can."

"Morning will be fine," Kit said. "What time?"

"Better wait until the fishing boats have gone out for the day," her dad advised. "No sense in going to the marina at its busiest time."

"Most of the boats leave between eight and nine o'clock," Kit said.

"Why don't I pick you up around nine-thirty, then?" Eric asked.

"Fine. Sounds great." Kit wished she could pull the last two words back. She hoped Eric understood that she meant great in a business sense, not in a social sense.

Eric rose. "I'd better be easing on down the road. I'm pleased to have met you, Mr. and Mrs. Cummings. And I'm really glad that you'll let Kit work with me. I'm hoping we can make it a profitable summer."

"I think your plan sounds promising," Mrs. Cummings said.

"I'll see you in the morning, Eric." Kit rose and walked around the house with Eric rather than going back through the kitchen and living room. "I'm really glad you stopped by. I'm glad we have an understanding about this morning and about the upcoming weeks."

Eric reached for Kit's hand. "Let's shake on it, Kit." He clenched her hand in a hearty grip. "Here's to success."

"Right. To success." Did she imagine it, or had Eric held her hand just a few instants longer than necessary? She couldn't be sure. Maybe it was just wishful thinking on her part. As she watched him walk down the street, she knew she had to squelch such wishful thinking. She and Eric were business partners, and that was all.

That night, Kit fell asleep thinking about Nita and Rafe as well as about Eric. She wondered what might develop from their business deal. That night, Eric had seemed so different from her first impression of him. He really wasn't a know-it-all braggart. No more than she was. Maybe they both had been trying to impress each other the day they met at the clinic. First impressions could be very erroneous.

The next morning, Kit rose early. Although her leg felt fine, she took time to give it a good soaking in a tub of hot water. If it weren't for the built-up shoe, she would have been almost able to forget about her leg and to erase the bad memories from her thinking like scribbles from a chalk board. But the shoe was there, a constant reminder. Before dressing in her jeans and T-shirt, she took ten minutes more to do the exercises her therapist had recommended. The therapist hoped that she would be able to discard the orthopedic shoe in time. How much time? He had been careful not to be too specific about that.

"Mom," Kit said as she entered the kitchen where her mother was shaking Wheaties into blue bowls. "I've got to do something about Rafe and all those condo flyers." Kit smiled. Her mother reminded her of Old Mother Hubbard in the mornings. She never wore an apron; she always wore a blue tent-shaped smock to protect her work clothes as she puttered about in the kitchen preparing breakfast.

"What do you have in mind?" Her mother set a blue pitcher of milk on the table.

"Maybe I could finish signing the ones Rafe left with me and leave them at the library. You know, on that table right inside the front entry where there are all kinds of freebie brochures about things to do and see in the keys. Do you think anyone would mind?"

"No, I don't think so. It might be a good idea. That way, only people who were really interested in a condo would bother to pick up a flyer. Want me to take them along as I go to work?"

"Would you, mom? I'd really appreciate it. I'll have to go to Casa Marina and tell Rafe what's come up about the fishing trips. He'll understand. And I could keep a supply of the flyers at the library if he wants me to."

"Sit down and eat some breakfast," her mother said.

"Can't, mom." Kit nodded toward the clock. "I'll mo-ped to the hotel and talk to Rafe personally. I'll try to get back here before Eric arrives."

"Your dad will be here to greet him if you're a few minutes late, Kit. But you'd better get going."

Kit grabbed her white helmet and the mo-ped keys and rode to the palm-shaded hotel on the other side of the island. Overhead, gulls wheeled and glided, and gentle waves lapped against the coral rock sea wall near the parking area. The smell of coffee permeated the salty breeze as she entered the coffee shop. Kit waved to Rafe and sat at a table in the corner away from the picture window that overlooked the sea. The shop was almost deserted, and

Rafe strolled to her, his tanned skin and dark hair contrasting with his white uniform.

"Nice to see you, Kit. Having breakfast?" He pulled out his order pad.

"I need to talk to you, Rafe. Why don't you bring me a glass of orange juice so it'll be legal and all. Don't want to get you fired."

"Sure thing." Rafe headed for the kitchen, and in a few minutes he returned with two frosty glasses of orange juice. He placed one in front of Kit, then sat across from her, sipping from the other glass.

"They don't mind you fraternizing with the customers?" Kit grinned at him as she tasted the sweet, tangy juice.

"I'm on break for fifteen minutes. I've been working since six o'clock."

Kit enjoyed a few more swallows of orange juice, then explained her job situation to Rafe. "Mom's taking the flyers to the library this morning, Rafe. Okay?"

"Good deal! Never thought of trying to appeal to the intelligentsia of the city. If you don't want to bother with the flyers, it's okay. I just thought that since you seemed sort of at loose ends for the summer—"

"Thanks for the thought, Rafe. And I'll keep on signing flyers to take to the library. I can do that and manage the fishing deal, too."

They were just finishing their orange juice when Eric entered the coffee shop and headed their way. Kit smiled and waved to him. That day he was wearing chinos and a copper-colored shirt that matched his hair, and he walked with a casual confidence that told Kit he was quite aware of his neat appearance. For a moment, she was surprised. She had thought that only girls planned their wardrobes so carefully. No doubt Eric was intent on making a good impression at the marinas they would be visiting.

"Eric, I want you to meet a friend of mine, Rafe Mira. Rafe works here, and I had to see him before we left for the marinas."

"Howdy." Eric nodded to Rafe coolly. Then he looked back at Kit. "Your dad told me you were here. He said to leave the mo-ped key with Rafe and he'll pick it up later in the day. We need to get going."

Kit glanced at her watch, surprised that it was well past nine-thirty. "Okay, Eric." She stood. "We'll see you, Rafe. Wish us luck on this business venture!"

"Luck!" Rafe said. "Lots of it!"

"Thanks, man," Eric replied, guiding Kit toward the door.

"Sorry I was late, Eric," Kit said.

"It's okay." Eric shrugged. "But we do need to get going. My brother wrote out a list of the marinas in the area." He held a sheet of paper toward Kit. "Which one should we try first?"

Kit scanned the list. "Our best bet would probably be to go to Stock Island. There are three marinas there, and all three have fairly good access to the flats."

"They all have tackle shops?"

"Yes. All three draw a good trade. At least that's what gramp says. Let's not try Sea Haven where we were yesterday. I don't like the idea of competing with gramp, okay?"

"Fine with me. How about the Gulfshore for starters?"

"Sounds good."

Eric drove past the White Street fishing pier, past Smathers Beach and on along the boulevard until they reached the intersection of U.S. Route 1. He followed the highway for about a mile, then turned right, following signs that pointed the way to the Gulfshore Marina.

"I'm going to let you do the talking," Kit said when they had parked the car near a weathered building. "It's your boat."

"Let's see how it goes." Eric opened the door to the dive and tackle shop and let Kit enter first; then they approached a steely-eyed, bald-headed man who seemed to be in charge of the shop, which smelled faintly of hemp rope and bait shrimp.

Eric cleared his throat. "Sir, we'd like to talk to you about using your marina as headquarters for our charter boat."

"What's your name?" the man asked, his sharp gaze scanning Eric's face.

"Eric Hartley. And this is my partner Kit Cummings. We work together."

"You Chet Cummings girl?" the man asked Kit.

"His granddaughter," Kit replied.

The man turned his attention back to Eric. "You got a license?"

Eric reached for his billfold and extracted his license. The man glanced at it briefly, then shook his head. "Sorry, kids. I've got captains working out of this marina who've been with me for years. This is the off-season. I just can't let anyone else move in. I do that and pretty soon there's not enough business to make it pay for anyone. You come back maybe during the season, okay?"

"Sure," Eric said. "Thanks for your time."

When they were back at the car, Kit sighed. "That was quick. Hope it's not going to be the story of our day."

Eric pulled out his list again. "How about trying the Jackson Marina?"

"Might as well." Kit felt let down. She didn't know what she had expected, but she guessed she had expected to be accepted at the first place they tried. Otherwise, why the let-down feeling?

Eric drove from the Gulfshore, followed the blacktop road past some mobile-home courts and then turned onto a marl-filled lane that led to the Jackson Marina and Dive Shop. The building had a fresh coat of green paint, and Kit tried not to let it remind her of the rehabilitation clinic.

"Maybe you should do the talking, Kit. You know your way around these places better than I do."

"No way. You're older. And you have the license."

They entered the dive shop, and this time Eric spoke to a middle-aged lady whose stout body was encased in a gray jump suit that gave her the look of a sturdy, salt-weathered dock piling. After assuring them that she was Mrs. Jackson and that she was in charge, she listened to their request.

"You kids look awfully young to be in the charter-boat business."

"I'm eighteen," Eric said. "Legal."

Kit kept quiet. No use advertising the fact she was only seventeen.

"A small boat suitable for the flats is going to be crowded with four people in it," Mrs. Jackson said.

"Maybe we'll just take out one person at a time," Kit said. "Lots of fishermen prefer to be the only customer."

"And lots of fishermen prefer to take a buddy along to split the fee," Mrs. Jackson said. She looked at Eric's license, then stared at both of them thoughtfully. "Why don't you come back tomorrow? Let me think it over. I like to sleep on a thing before I make a final decision."

"Fine, Mrs. Jackson," Eric said. "We'll get back to you tomorrow."

Again, Kit felt a sense of defeat. When they were out of the shop, she turned to Eric. "What are we going to do now?"

"Well, we're not going to sit around waiting for Mrs. Jackson to make up her mind. Let's go on to the next place on the list." He backed from their parking slot and headed on up the highway to the Coral Cove Marina. There the office was made of coral rock, and Kit welcomed the cool dankness of the interior where they found a young sunburned man on duty. The name tag on his shirt announced that he was Red Huggins. Again, Eric presented their plan.

"Sometimes I do believe in fate," Red said, tugging on his ear lobe. "Just this very morning one of my best guides left me. The wife's going to take him on a grand tour of Europe. Got nobody special to fill his spot."

"We'll be glad to fill it for you," Eric said. "How many boats go out from here?"

91

"Only two. One, with Hap Horner away. You'd make the second."

Kit felt some qualms of doubt. Most marinas had lots of charter boats working from their docks. Maybe nobody came here looking for a boat to charter. But she kept quiet.

"Got a license?"

Eric produced his license once more. "Got a sound boat. Good tackle. And Kit's had lots of experience guiding boats in the area."

"What's your last name again, Kit?"

"Cummings. I've worked with my grandfather on the *Sea Sprite*."

"I know your grandfather, Kit. Why, I've even been out fishing with him. Couple of years ago. Sure thing." Red smiled broadly. "Tell you what. Why don't you get some business cards made up? Put your name on them along with the name of this place—Coral Cove Marina. Bring them out here for distribution and you'll be in business."

"How long does it take to have cards printed?" Kit asked.

"A few days, I suppose," Red said.

"We wanted to get started right away," Eric said. "Like tomorrow, for instance."

"Don't know about that." Red shrugged and tugged on his ear lobe again. "Just depends on who shows up and how bad they want to fish. Leave your name and number with me. I'll post them on the bulletin board. Something just may come up for you."

Kit jotted the information in bold black letters on the paper Red gave her, and they watched while he posted it on the cork board next to his cash register.

"Thanks, Mr. Huggins," Eric said. "We appreciate your vote of confidence."

"Call me Red, Eric." He smiled at them. "You too, Kit. And tell your granddad hey for me, you hear?"

"Will do," Kit replied.

Once they were back in Eric's car, they grinned at each other, excited by their success. "This calls for a celebration," Eric said. Then, in mock seriousness, he asked, "Miss Cummings, are you free for a celebration?"

"Why how nice of you to inquire, Mr. Hartley. It just happens that I'm free as the breeze, and I'd love to celebrate with you."

Eric backed the car into the scanty marina driveway, then headed toward the highway. When they were on the straightaway once more, he reached for Kit's hand and squeezed it.

Kit returned the squeeze, hardly thinking about the other girl in Eric's life. They were business partners; they had just taken their first step forward together, and he was holding her hand. Kit said nothing, afraid that speech might break the spell that had suddenly brought them together.

7

Eric withdrew his hand from Kit's, placing it on the steering wheel, and she reached up on the pretext of smoothing her hair. His next words snapped her from her state of euphoria, and her feeling of closeness to him vanished immediately.

"What we need to do first," Eric said, "is to go to a printer and order some business cards."

"Right," she agreed. "Where shall we go?"

"You know Key West better than I do. Any suggestions?"

"There are a couple of places on Fleming Street. We could stop by my house and do some telephoning, some comparison shopping."

"And maybe we could sketch out a sample card. We need to decide what we want our card to say."

"Right," Kit agreed. "Good idea."

Eric drove directly to Kit's house, and once they were inside, she handed him the telephone directory while she brought out pen and paper.

"Why don't you do the calling, Eric? You can jot down the figures on this scratch pad."

Eric made the calls and asked for the price of a ream of cards. "Printers Unlimited offers the best deal, Kit."

"Then that's where we'll go." She pulled out a chair at the kitchen table and invited Eric to sit down. "Let's decide what the card will need to say. We want it to be attractive. It'll be our only sales tool."

"Right."

Kit began sketching smiling faces across the top of the page. Under them she wrote: Have a Nice Day—Go Fishing. Under that in smaller letters she wrote: Aboard the *Starfish*. Then, on the next two lines, she wrote: Captain Eric Hartley, Guide Kit Cummings.

"So far you're doing fine," Eric said. "Now we need to specify the type of fishing we'll offer. No deep-water jigging. No trolling in the gulf. What about writing: Backwater fishing on protected flats?"

"Good deal." Kit jotted down the words. "That's exactly what we'll be doing, and the word *protected* should attract people who don't usually fish but who might like to go out for a day just to try their hand at it if they thought it was safe."

Eric pulled the paper toward him and penned in: Daily charters 8:00 A.M.–4:00 P.M. "Okay?"

"Looks good to me. Now whose phone number shall we include? We'll need two numbers, I think.

On the left, let's put the number of the marina and on the right—"

Eric looked at her as she hesitated. "What's the matter?"

Kit shrugged and doodled on the paper. "The person whose number appears on the card is going to have to stick close to the telephone in order not to miss any calls. That could turn into a drag."

"No problem, Kit. Let's put my number on the card. My brother has an answering device that he connects to his telephone when nobody's home. It allows the caller to leave a message. Henry has to be at sea most of the day, so this gadget is a must for him."

"And he won't mind if we get calls on it, too?"

"I don't think so. He never gets enough calls to use up all the recording space, and I doubt that we will, either. I'll check with him, but let's go ahead and use my phone number."

"Then let's take this to the printer and see what he thinks. He may have some suggestions that we haven't thought of."

They drove the few blocks down Fleming Street toward town, parked in front of the print shop and went inside. Kit let Eric do the talking, backing him up with ideas and suggestions when necessary. In just a few minutes, they had placed their order and arranged to pick up the cards a few days later.

"Guess that sign we left at the marina will have to do as our advertising until the cards are ready," Eric said.

"Guess so. Hope someone sees it. Today. I'm really eager to get this business started. Jeepers,

Eric, if business is good, I could have enough money for a boat before the summer ends. I really could."

"Don't count your coconuts before they fall from the tree," Eric advised. "We've both got to remember that summer is a slow season. We may be lucky to get one or two charters a week."

Kit's brain began to work like an adding machine. "But that would be lots of bucks, Eric. Big Bucks. A high-rent operation."

"It could be. I just don't want to be disappointed, so I try to look at the business from all angles. Don't forget that we'll have expenses, too."

"Yeah. The cards, for starters. And gasoline. And oil. And tackle."

"And let's celebrate before you think of anything else, like motor overhauls, boat repairs, broken poling poles."

Kit looked at Eric, saw a twinkle in his eye, and knew he was teasing. "Enough yet. How shall we celebrate?"

"Think of something you've always wanted to do but never have done. Something within reason, of course."

Kit thought. She could think of a jillion things. She would like to walk on the moon. She would like to fish off Dry Tortugas in her own boat. But she tried to think of something reasonable.

"There's something I've always wanted to do," Eric said after he had waited for Kit to speak up.

"What?"

"I've always wanted to eat all the key lime pie I could hold. Do you like key lime pie?"

"Love it. Shall we celebrate with a pie? We could bring it to my place and pig out on the patio."

"Or we could take it to my place," Eric said. "There's a patio there, too. We live in an apartment house, but we have use of the patio. Let's go, Kit. I'm starving."

They drove to the bakery and went in together. Kit insisted on paying half of the bill. "Partners," she reminded him. "Fifty-fifty. Starting right now."

They paid for the pie and drove toward Eric's house. He parked the car and nodded toward an old white-frame home. "There it is."

"It's very similar to my house, isn't it?"

"It doesn't have a widow's walk," Eric pointed out. "And it needs a coat of paint. But it does have a hollow tree in the front yard that was supposed to be a hiding place for pirate loot back in the days of sailing ships and freebooters."

"Really? I want to see it."

"Come take a look." Eric led the way to a sprawling fig tree with an oval-shaped hole in its trunk. "I've taken a flashlight and searched inside the cavity for any stray doubloons, but no luck."

Kit examined the tree, then followed Eric around the house to a shaded tropical garden surrounded by a Croton hedge that made an excellent privacy screen. The red-bricked patio had been swept clean, and Eric set the pie on a wrought-iron table near a small pool where lily pads and yellow waxlike blossoms covered most of the water's surface.

"Hang tight for a sec and I'll get some plates and forks." Eric disappeared inside the back door, and Kit sat at the table. Eric's back yard was more of a tropical garden than was her own. Bougainvilleas climbed and twined up a palm tree, leaving a trail of pink blossoms, and in one corner of the garden, she could count six varieties of cacti. Hibiscus bushes with golden and pink blossoms grew in another corner. The moist earthy smell of the garden seemed redolent of growth.

"Who takes care of all this?" Kit asked when Eric returned. "It must be a full-time job."

"Our landlady takes care of it. It's her hobby. She's especially proud of her orchids." Eric nodded toward a bed of orchids that Kit hadn't had time to notice.

"Where does she live?"

"Upstairs. We rent the downstairs. She likes to be up high where she has a view of the sea from her window." Eric set out two paper plates, two forks and two napkins. Then he cut the pie with the side of a serving spatula, lifting a large slice onto Kit's plate. "How's that for starters?"

"Super. Really super." Kit watched while Eric slid a piece of pie onto his own plate; then they began eating. She started out taking dainty bites, savoring the tart sweetness, feeling the creamy filling melt on her tongue, but Eric gulped his first piece in about ten seconds and was helping himself to a second slice.

"You really do like pie."

"I warned you." Eric laughed. "The first time Dian served me a piece, I could hardly believe it was lime pie. I had heard about it, of course, but I expected it to be green, not cream colored."

Dian. Dian. The name all but exploded in Kit's mind, and she could hardly keep her thoughts on what Eric was saying. Was Dian his girl friend? Was she the misty blonde who had been with him at Mallory?

"Kit?" Eric paused, looking at her questioningly. "Are you okay?"

She forced her mind back to the present, back to Eric's words. "Sure I'm okay. Just thinking about how good the pie is. Some cafés do color it green, you know. Dad says they're afraid the tourists won't believe it's really key lime if it isn't green."

Kit ate two pieces of pie and didn't mind at all that Eric ate the other four. When he finished, he gave a long sigh. "That was the greatest. The very greatest. Are you sure you had enough?"

"Positive." Kit laughed. She wished she could think of a reason for staying in the lovely tropical garden longer, but she couldn't. And she guessed that Eric wouldn't want her to linger. What if Dian just accidentally stopped by and found her here? She wondered if Eric had told Dian about their charter business? It would take a pretty broad-minded girl friend not to object to her guy's starting a business with another girl, especially a business that would throw them together for hours at a time. Of course Dian would know that Eric would always be chaperoned by whoever chartered the *Starfish* for the day.

"I'd better be going," Kit said at last. "I'd offer to help with the dishes, but I guess that won't be necessary." She gathered up the paper plates and napkins, then handed Eric the forks and the serving spatula. Eric carried the utensils inside, then returned to drive her home. When he stopped the car in front of her house, Kit got out before he could come around and open the door for her. They were business partners. No point in acting as if she were his date for the afternoon.

"I think we accomplished a lot of business today, Eric. Now all we have to do is to wait for a call from the marina."

"I'll let you know the minute I hear anything about a charter," Eric promised. "In the meantime, I'll be readying some more tackle. And I'll study some charts of the backwater areas. That might help me catch on more quickly as to where the deepwater channels are. Guess I'd better pick up some tide tables, too."

It was on the tip of Kit's tongue to offer to help Eric with the charts and tables, but she kept still. They were business partners, and charts and tide tables could be dealt with during their business hours.

"See you, Eric," she called over her shoulder as she headed for her front door, walking carefully to avoid limping. Eric waved and drove on down the street.

Eric seemed to take her enthusiasm with him as he left. A business that had seemed to offer many bright prospects a few minutes earlier now seemed to offer only disappointment. What if nobody called? What if they took someone out and that someone didn't get even one strike after a whole day on the water? The pine stair treads creaked as she hurried to the bathroom to run a tub of hot water before other business pitfalls occurred to her. She read a recent issue of *Saltwater Sportsman* as she soaked her leg. Professional writers always made fishing sound so supereasy. They seldom alluded to the skill and the patience that went into actually catching and boating a fish.

After she had soaked her leg for thirty minutes, she dressed in clean slacks and shirt and began her exercises. She sat on the edge of her bed, slipped her foot through the padded leather thong on the five-pound weight and began lifting and lowering her leg. Five pounds didn't seem like much of a weight, but her leg muscles soon tired. Even at that, she was able to lift the weight three more times than she had lifted it the day before. That showed progress.

Kit rested for the remainder of the afternoon, and that evening, after an early supper, she took the condo flyers to the dock and passed them out to whomever she could get to take one. No use missing a chance to make a little extra as long as she and Eric weren't actually working yet. She half expected to see Rafe at the dock, but he didn't show up. Maybe he had been allowed to work the dinner hour at Casa Marina. That was his hope. That's when a waiter earned big tips, working the dinner hour.

As she strolled along the dock, Kit kept her gaze on the water, on the boats coming in for the evening. Would she see Eric and Miss Misty there again? Dian. He had called her Dian as casually as if Kit were well acquainted with her. Dian. Again, Kit realized how much she missed Anita. It was a drag not having anyone to talk over her problems with. Anita would have had advice for her concerning Eric and Dian; she always seemed to know the best thing to do. How was she going to get along without her for the whole summer!

Kit spent most of the next three days sitting within

earshot of the telephone. What if Eric tried to call when she was out? But she really didn't have any reason to go out. None at all. So she sat at home. She cleaned the kitchen cupboards for her mother, replacing the old shelf paper with new and washing the dishes on the top shelves, dishes that they seldom used. Dullsville.

About four in the afternoon of the third day, she rode her mo-ped to the bight where the big party boats docked with their all-day passengers. Stationing herself near the *Can't Miss,* she passed out condo flyers to the people coming off the boat. Then she watched as the boat's crew began tossing fish from the holding tank. Kingfish; pompano; snapper; grouper. Nothing very large. She wandered on along the dock, noting the day's catch. One trolling boat had brought in a five-foot marlin, and a huge crowd had gathered around to view it, to take pictures.

"Any calls?" she asked her dad when she returned home.

"No, Kit. You expecting a call?"

"Come on, dad. You know Eric and I are about to die for someone to hire us for a day on the flats."

Her father chuckled. "Well, you know how it is—summertime. I just talked to your grandfather."

"Did he go out today?"

"Yes. Had a good day. Caught enough 'cuda to keep the customer happy, and then to top off the day, they caught a thirty-pound permit."

"I'm glad the fish were biting. Maybe tomorrow we'll get a call."

"I'm wishing you luck," her dad said.

The phone didn't ring all evening, and although

Kit tried not to be disappointed, she had secretly hoped Eric would call her just to say—well, to say anything or nothing at all. She considered calling him, then discarded that idea. What if he were out with Dian? She didn't want his brother to think Eric had formed a partnership with a girl who was going to be calling the house all the time, tying up his business phone.

Three days passed before Eric called her. She had been wondering if he had been spending his time fishing for black-tip, trying to beat her tournament record, but she didn't risk asking. And now his news was so good that she forgot all about the hours she had spent fretting and waiting.

"We've got a charter, Kit. Tomorrow. One woman. All day. There's just one catch."

"What?"

"She's determined to catch bonefish, and I remember what you said about taking a person out for one kind of fish only."

"Did you try to talk up 'cuda? Shark?"

"Sure. She has received citations for releasing every kind of game fish except bonefish, and this is what she wants to go after."

"Gross. Really gross. We can't make promises like that."

"Mellow out, Kit. Would you rather I had turned her down?"

"Of course not! If she wants bones, we'll do our best to find the bones."

"You know any secret spots?"

"Maybe. We'll see. What time are we leaving?"

"Nine o'clock. Eight was too early for her, but

we'd better be at the dock by eight, don't you think?"

"Yes. We'll need to see that everything is in order. We don't want any slip-ups on this first time out. Word-of-mouth advertising is very important in this business, Eric. Your person tells other people his experiences. That's the way a guide's reputation grows."

"Hey, I got the cards. They look just great. I've posted a few on some grocery-store bulletin boards in town, the library, the tourist info headquarters at Mallory."

"Swell." Kit tried not to sound disappointed, but she wondered why Eric hadn't called her to help with the posting of the cards. Or had Dian volunteered for the job! She tried to forget that possibility.

"I'll pick you up about ten minutes before eight tomorrow morning," Eric said. "Sound all right?"

"I'll be waiting. See you then." Kit replaced the receiver in its cradle, then turned to her parents. "We've got a charter. We've got one. Tomorrow! A woman after bonefish."

"Good luck, Kit," her mother said. "I hope everything goes well for you."

Kit thought she wouldn't be able to sleep at all that night, but she did. And she awakened the next morning feeling rested and eager for a day on the flats. She dressed in chinos and a tan T-shirt, although she knew she would be more comfortable in shorts. She sighed. She wasn't ready to bare her leg to public view just yet.

She ate cereal and toast and drank orange juice

and milk. She knew she needed a good breakfast for starters. Sometimes she got so excited about the fishing that she forgot all about lunch. And many times it was hard to stop for lunch because time was needed to get from one fishing grounds to another before changing tides spoiled the chances for a catch.

"Good luck, Kit," her dad called as she waved good-bye and walked toward Eric's Ford, which had stopped at the curb in front of the house. She smiled as she noted Eric's clothes—chinos and a tan T-shirt. They really did look like partners.

"Where's your boat?" she asked.

"It's at the marina. I took it out last night and rented a mooring."

"Good idea. Where do you usually keep it?"

"Henry lets me dock it with his boat, but I wanted to be sure to have it at the marina and in working order last night so there wouldn't be any delays this morning."

"Good thinking."

"You do know some bonefishing spots, don't you?" Eric studied her seriously.

"Yes. There are some special channels that should pay off for us if we're lucky."

They left the car some distance from the Coral Cove Marina, then walked to the office. Even before Red Huggins introduced them, Kit knew that the slightly built middle-aged woman standing near the Coke machine was their customer. She wore an expensive khaki-colored jump suit and deck shoes, and a wide-brimmed Panama hat sat at a jaunty angle on her auburn hair. She looked like a role model for the keys' best-dressed tourist, but she also looked businesslike, as if her business were fishing.

"Captain Hartley, ma'am," Eric said, offering his hand to the woman. "And this is your guide, Kit Cummings." Kit offered her hand along with a smile. She liked the woman's firm handshake.

"Good morning, Eric, Kit," the woman replied. "I'm Mrs. McGinnis. Maggie. Just call me Maggie. I don't hold with formalities. Are we ready to go?"

Kit stood straighter as she heard Maggie's voice. A blue-chip voice, gramp would have called it. The lady had class.

"We're just about ready." Eric looked pointedly at his watch. "You're a bit early, Mrs. McGinnis."

"Maggie. I know I said nine o'clock, but I couldn't wait. I figured you'd get here early, so I came on out."

"Fine," Eric said. "I'll bring the boat around, check the motors and equipment, pick up some bait. We'll soon be on our way."

"I've brought the lunch." Maggie picked up a canvas bag that had been sitting at her feet. "Ham and cheese sandwiches. Potato chips. Cokes."

"Sounds good." Kit took the lunch. "I'll pack it in the refrigerator compartment."

Kit went with Eric to get the boat and bring it to the dock near the marina office where their customer could board easily. She was relieved when both motors started on the first try. Eric checked the radio. It was working. "I'll go get the bait, Eric."

"What do we need?" he asked.

"I'm going to pick up some soft-shell crabs; maybe some squid."

Later, when they were ready to go, Kit helped Maggie step over the gunwale and settle herself in the fishing chair. Now she noted that Maggie had brought her own tackle.

"I always bring my own tackle," Maggie said, following Kit's gaze. "I like to fish with gear I'm used to."

"What have you brought?" Kit hated the thought of bringing in an unhappy customer at the end of the day just because that customer had used tackle unsuitable for the job.

"I've brought along a six-and-a-half-foot, five-ounce bass rod," Maggie said. "You see, that's what I use back in Iowa for fresh-water fishing. I inquired before coming down to the keys. Experts said this was suitable for bonefishing."

Kit nodded and breathed a small sigh of relief. Maggie was right. She had brought appropriate equipment.

"I've also brought a medium-weight spinning reel with a deep spool. It's loaded with eight-pound test monofilament line. I've heard that the average-size bonefish will run six to eight pounds."

Again, Kit nodded, but she knew the woman would be lucky if she caught a bone that big. She was more likely to catch in the three- to four-pound range. "I'll tie on a flat, quarter-ounce jig, Maggie."

"Why?"

"The flat jig holds the bait upright and helps keep it from hanging up on the turtle grass."

"I see." Maggie watched while Kit readied her tackle. Then they left the marina, traveling very slowly, leaving no wake until they were away from the dock area and in open water.

"You've got a good day for it," Kit said. "Lots of sunshine and not too much wind."

"Where are we going?" Maggie asked.

"We'll try some flats around Old Man Key first," Kit said. "If we don't spot fish there, we'll still have time to make a run to another flat where I sometimes have good luck."

Kit headed for a deep channel and opened the motor. They pounded across the sea, the bow of the boat knifing up a salty spray that misted over their faces. As soon as they neared their destination, Kit cut the motor and nodded to Eric. "Over there." She pointed.

Eric took the pole from the gunwale and climbed to the platform while Kit eased forward, wiped the salt spray from her sunglasses with her shirt tail and stood on the bow.

"Where shall I stand?" Maggie asked.

"You're fine right where you are for the moment," Kit said. "I'll try to spot some fish for you; then you can stand up here and cast. Or maybe you'd like to stand up here with me right now and I can show you what to look for."

Maggie hoisted herself onto the bow. "I've read a lot about fishing for bones, but I've never had any experience."

Kit checked again to make sure Maggie's tackle was ready for action. "The tide's at low ebb, Maggie, and right now's a good time to scan the surface for tailing fish. They swim onto this flat to feed on crabs, shrimp, mollusks that they find on the bottom. If the bones are here, they'll be so intent on their feeding that they may not see us. Watch the surface for protruding tails."

The three of them scanned the water, seeing nothing but the reflection of clouds in the silvery undulating brine. Now and then, the bottom of the boat dragged on the sand, and Eric had to exert all his strength to keep them moving. At last, Kit sighed. "That's enough of that. The water's getting too deep now to show tails even if there were any."

"Now what?" Maggie asked.

"Now we watch for puffs of mud in the water. And we'll watch for a wake on the surface. You see, a school of bonefish may mosey along very slowly while feeding, but a fisherman can usually see a telltale wake behind the school if the water is smooth."

"This water isn't very smooth anymore," Maggie said. "The wind's up. I don't think I could make out a wake. Too many ripples."

"You're right," Kit said. "So we'll look for mud puffs beneath the surface. When the bones feed, they nose into the sand and marl. You may see puffs of sand and mud, or you may see a generalized cloudiness which may cover a large area."

They looked closely and intently all the while Eric was poling the boat across the flats. After two hours, Maggie began to glance at her watch. "Time's getting away from us. Perhaps we should try a different location?"

"All right," Kit agreed. "We'll make a run."

"How about a snack first?" Maggie asked.

Kit tried to be tactful. "Maggie, the tide here is constantly growing higher, but I know a spot quite a ways off where we can still get in on part of the low tide if we hurry. It'll be too late if we take time to eat."

"All right, then. Forget eating. I just thought you kids might be hungry."

Kids. Kit tried not to resent the word, but it did detract from the professional image they were trying to build for themselves.

"Everyone down and braced for a long run," Kit said. "This will take about fifteen minutes, and we'll be traveling fast. "Hang onto your hats." She waited until Eric was seated in the stern and Maggie was settled in the fishing chair before she opened the motor wide. Again, they raced across the sea, moving faster than the clouds, faster than the gulls wheeling directly overhead. Kit usually didn't like to travel at such high speed, but it was the only way of reaching the flat near Marl Key while the tide was still fairly low. When at last they arrived at their destination, she was glad to cut the motor, to enjoy the sudden silence. And it relieved her to see no other fishing boats in the vicinity. This was a spot she frequently fished with her grandfather, and she wouldn't have been surprised to have found him already testing the area.

Eric poled them across the flats for almost thirty minutes with no sign of fish. Kit reached into the bait sack, crumbled some crab and shell in her hands, then flung it into the water about thirty feet from their boat.

"Why did you do that?" Maggie asked.

"There's a deep channel out there that the bones sometimes use as they swim onto the flats. They can smell food from a great distance. Thought maybe I could entice them right to our boat."

But the idea didn't work. No bonefish came to investigate the chum in the water. Eric continued poling silently across the vast expanse of flats until Kit motioned for him to stop. She pointed to the bottom.

"See those brown marks on the bottom?" she asked. "Fish have been here. Recently." As she studied the water, she felt her heart race. She kept her voice low, but the urgency of her words came through. "They're down below us now. See the wake! See it!"

Maggie peered where Kit was pointing. Silently, she nodded and prepared to cast. Eric plunged the pole deep into the sand and tied the boat to it with a stern line. Maggie cast across the school, and Kit saw her bait hit bottom.

"Give it a couple of jerks in the mud, Maggie," Kit said softly.

Maggie jerked the rod slightly, and a fish hit the lure. The fight was on.

The reel screamed a protest as line shot out, and the hooked fish streaked some four hundred feet across the flats before he slowed down.

"It's hard to believe any fish can travel that fast," Maggie said.

"Don't talk," Kit shouted, forgetting to be tactful. "Reel him in. Wind. Wind."

Maggie fought the fish for almost twenty minutes and at last brought it in. Kit held the landing net, and they admired the silver, glistening body. Eric helped weigh the fish, which ran right at four pounds.

"You want to keep it or release it," Kit asked, hoping for release.

"I always release the fish," Maggie said. "But you will be witness to the catch, right?"

"Right." Kit removed the barb from the fish's mouth, kneeling at the gunwale as she held it in the water just below the surface for a few moments to allow it time to recover from the shock of the catch and the fight. Then she released it and watched it dart across the flats toward deep water.

"Want to try again?" Kit asked.

"No," Maggie said. "Take me in, please."

Kit looked at Eric and saw an almost imperceptible squinting of his left eye as he shrugged. What had gone wrong? The woman had wanted to catch a bonefish. She had caught a bonefish. But now, although the day was only half over, she was asking to go in. Kit pushed her glasses onto the top of her head for a few seconds while she thought, but there really was nothing to think about. She perched the glasses back on her nose and pointed the boat toward the marina, feeling a sudden chill of defeat and foreboding.

8

Nobody spoke as Kit eased the *Starfish* to the marina dock. Although she couldn't see Maggie McGinnis's face, Kit could see her sitting stiff as the spine on a sea urchin. She had barely moved since they left the flats. What had gone wrong! What had made her decide to give up the last half of her fishing day? If she gave Red Huggins a negative report on their work, Red might tell them to find another marina. After she cut the motor, Eric stepped over the gunwale quickly, ready to offer Maggie a steadying hand. Kit waited in the boat, expecting the worst.

"Would you prefer your money in cash or traveler's check?" Maggie asked as she and Eric headed for the marina office.

"Cash, please," Eric replied.

Kit looped a line around a dock cleat, climbed

from the boat and joined Eric and Maggie in the office where the coral-rock coolness matched Maggie's mood. Kit stood a bit to one side as Maggie prepared to pay, and Kit sensed Red and another man watching the scene from near the cash register. Would Maggie offer only a half day's pay for the charter she had reserved for a full day? Kit felt an angry tightness in her throat.

"Here you go, kids." Maggie pulled four crisp fifty-dollar bills and an extra twenty from her handbag. "The charter price plus a tip."

"But . . . but . . ." Kit stammered as she looked at the bills.

"Is something wrong?" Maggie asked.

"No. No, not at all," Kit said. "It's just that . . ." She felt herself flushing. "It's just that I thought you were unhappy about something. I mean you hired us for all day."

"I got what I went out for, Kit. I wanted to catch a bonefish, and that's what I did. I was so awed by the experience, by the speed and beauty of that fish, that I wanted to hold onto the memory for as long as possible. I wanted to do nothing else that would distract me from the main event of the day, from one of the peak moments of my life."

"Oh!" Kit and Eric spoke in unison; then Kit felt herself flushing even more deeply.

"I'm sorry if I gave the impression that I was displeased. The truth lies in the opposite direction. I was overwhelmed."

"We're glad," Eric said. "Maybe you'd like to go out again sometime. Will you be here long?"

"I'm flying to New York early tomorrow morning," Maggie said. "But the next time I come to the

keys, I'll be sure to ask for you and Kit. Now, let's
get on with the paper work involved in the catch, the
release, the citation."

Red pulled the form from a file, and Eric filled it
out, showing that Maggie McGinnis caught a four-
pound bonefish and released it. Eric and Kit signed
the form. Maggie signed it. And Red placed it in an
envelope for mailing.

"Done!" Eric said. "You should receive a citation
certificate within a few weeks. If you don't, let us
know, and we'll find out why." He gave her one of
their business cards, and as she slipped it into her
billfold, a plump, elderly man who had been standing beside Red, watching and listening to their
conversation, approached Kit, his hands thrust
deeply into the pockets of his polyester leisure suit.

"Is the *Starfish* booked for tomorrow?" he asked.

"No," Kit replied. "We're free. Are you interested in going out with us for a day's fishing?"

"Yes, I am. Bonefish! That's what I'm after, too.
I'd like to tie into a twelve-pounder out there in that
thin water."

"We never make promises about the catch," Kit
said. "Some days the bones hit, and some days they
don't." She grinned. "That's why they call the sport
fishing instead of catching."

"Got a real sense of humor there, haven't you,
girlie?" The man's stomach shook as he chuckled.
"A real sense of humor."

Kit tried not to flinch at being called girlie. *The
customer is always right.* Then Eric spoke up.

"We could make a good try at putting you in
position to catch a bonefish, sir. Would you like to
book the *Starfish* for tomorrow?"

"I sure would. Let me have one of your cards."

Eric gave him a card, and he jotted his name on the back of it, then returned it to Eric. "What time do we leave?"

"Eight o'clock, Mr. Barkus," Eric replied, reading his name from the card.

"You'll furnish the tackle?" Mr. Barkus asked.

"Right," Kit replied.

"I'll see you right here, then," he said.

"Fine," Kit replied. She and Eric left the Coral Cove office and headed toward the *Starfish*. "Hey! What a deal, Eric! Two charters right in a row! I told you word-of-mouth advertising would help us as much as anything."

"I'm really glad Maggie McGinnis was pleased. She had me guessing there for a while."

"Yeah, me, too." Kit helped Eric hose down the boat, wipe it dry and ease it to its overnight mooring; then they went to Eric's car. When they were on their way home, Eric reached for Kit's hand, squeezed it for a moment and then continued to hold it. She returned his squeeze, making no effort to remove her hand from his grasp.

"We make a good team, Kit."

"Agreed." Kit wondered if he meant a business team or some other kind of team. He was holding her hand. Quite definitely, he was holding her hand. And she liked the warmth of his touch. They drove on in a companionable silence until they reached Kit's house.

"See you in the morning, Kit." Eric smiled as he placed both hands on the steering wheel.

"Fine. I'll be ready." Kit left the car with mixed emotions. Eric acted as if he really liked her, as if their partnership might be growing into something more than just a business deal. Yet he knew she had a free afternoon, and he had not suggested that they might do something together. She wished she could read his mind. She wished she had Anita to talk to. She wanted to look back at the departing car, but she refrained from doing so.

At supper that evening, Kit told her parents of the day's success. Her grandfather had joined them, and he rejoiced with her.

"I'm pleased for you, Kit," he said in his gravelly voice. "I really am. I'm just sorry the two of us couldn't work together this summer. You're not overdoing, not overworking that leg, are you?"

"No way, gramp. I did man the pole for a while, and I'm going to try to increase my platform time a few minutes each day. But I stopped before my leg began to hurt. I feel fine."

After supper, Kit took her warm bath, exercised her leg and went to bed early. The day on the water hadn't overtaxed her leg, but she felt more tired than she had realized earlier. And in spite of having worn a sun screen on her face, her skin felt hot and sunburned. She patted lotion on it and hoped she wouldn't burn and peel. She seldom got a sunburn, but her weeks in the hospital had made her skin very vulnerable.

The next morning, she was waiting on the front porch, enjoying the trade wind when Eric stopped for her. She smiled. Although they hadn't planned it, they were both wearing jeans and gingham shirts. Their minds seemed to operate on the same wave length.

"Feeling lucky?" Kit asked as she slid onto the car seat beside him.

"Think we can have two good days in a row?"

"No reason why not." She eyed Eric's face, noting that he, too, had taken some sun the day before. His tan had a definite ruddy cast, and a smattering of freckles paraded across the bridge of his nose. Even his coppery hair seemed a bit sun bleached. But the added color enhanced his looks, made the green glints in his hazel eyes all the more noticeable.

"What are you thinking?" Eric asked.

Kit looked away quickly, glad he couldn't read her thoughts. "I was still thinking about how lucky we are to have another charter for today. Wouldn't it be great if it would work out like that for us every day—someone always waiting at the marina to sign up for the next day."

"Dream on, girl. Dream on."

"Yeah, I know it's nothing but a dream. But it could happen, Eric. It really could."

After parking in the shade of a sea grape tree out of the way of marina customers, Kit helped Eric ready the boat. They filled the gasoline tank, wiped the dew from the seats and the gunwale and shooed a friendly pelican from the poling platform. Eric tested the motors and the radio.

"All set," he said at last. "Wonder where good old Joe Barkus is."

"Maybe he overslept. But I don't understand how a guy could oversleep on a morning when he was going fishing. I always wake up ahead of time."

"That's because you have salt water in your veins instead of blood." Eric raised the lid on the refriger-

119

ator compartment. "Hey, look! We forgot to offload yesterday's lunch."

"It'll still be good, won't it? I mean it was on ice all night, wasn't it?"

"Sure. If Mr. Barkus hasn't already bought lunch, we can suggest using this stuff."

Kit left the dock and walked through the marina office, looking in the parking lot to see if their customer was approaching. She waited for a few minutes, then strolled back to the boat.

"Maybe he forgot, Eric. Maybe we should call him."

Eric pulled the card from his pocket. "He didn't leave us an address or a phone number. Just his name."

"I'll see if he's in the book," Kit said. "He might be a local." She looked up the name in the telephone directory but found no Barkus listed. "I suppose I could call some motels and see if he's registered."

"That'd take forever." Eric shook his head. "And it'd tie up Red's phone."

Just then, a young couple approached them. "You have a boat for hire today?" the man asked. "We'd like to go out, if you're available."

"Sorry, sir," Kit said, "but we're booked for today."

"But wait," Eric said as the man turned away. "Our customer hasn't shown up yet. He's already a half hour late."

"How long will you wait for him?" the man asked.

"It's not fair to leave before nine-thirty," Kit said. "At least that's the rule gramp uses. He always waits an hour and a half for a customer before he makes other plans."

The man shook his head. "No deal. If we wait another hour, the tide will have changed. We'll have missed out on a lot of the best fishing time."

Kit knew the man was right, and she was tempted to forget Mr. Barkus and go with the couple who were present. Eric drew her aside, his left eye squinting slightly.

"Why don't we go with this couple? A bird in the hand, you know."

"If we do that and Mr. Barkus shows up ten seconds after we leave, he could ruin our reputation with his complaints." Kit sighed. "I don't think we should take the chance. We don't know anything about Joe Barkus. He may be testing us or something. He may have lots of buddies just waiting to get the word from him on our reliability. If we get a bad reputation, then that reflects on the marina, too."

"Okay. So we wait it out. I know you're right. I just hate to see a live one slip through our fingers."

They waited until nine-thirty, but Mr. Barkus didn't show up. "Rotten luck!" Kit groaned. "Why couldn't he have called us? Not only did we lose our day with him, but we also lost a second chance to go out."

"I think we've learned a lesson, Kit. From now on, get a deposit before we reserve the boat for anyone. That should eliminate the problem." His lips pressed into a thin line.

"Gramp has never done that." Kit wondered if she should argue, knowing Eric was angry.

"Does he lose many days to no-shows?"

"Sometimes," Kit admitted. "But he thinks a

121

showing of good will and good faith pays off in the long run."

"I don't have as long to run as he has," Eric said. "I need college tuition by mid-August. From now on, I'm for asking for some money down."

"Okay by me, I guess. We do have a time limit. For us, a day lost this summer is a day we'll never recover." She sighed. "Guess we're through for now. Might as well go home."

"The boat's gassed up," Eric said, relaxing. "We've got a lunch. I've no plans for the day, have you?"

"No, I suppose not." Kit tried to make her voice sound casual, but she felt her pulse thumping in her left temple. And she remembered how Eric had held her hand the day before.

"Why don't we go out for the day, Kit?"

Kit hesitated, wondering if Eric were really asking to spend a day with her just for fun. Thoughts of Miss Misty Dian flashed through her mind. But before she could answer, Eric spoke again.

"I mean, you could show me some of your fishing places, and I could mark them on this new chart I bought. I really need to be learning the territory, and this might be a good chance."

"Okay. That's a good idea." Kit didn't know if she was glad or sorry that Eric had immediately turned their day into a work project. She disliked moving in on another girl's territory, but she had to admit she was glad she would be spending the day with Eric for whatever reason.

"Why don't you go home and get on your swim suit?" Eric asked. "We can stop somewhere and have a swim before lunch. We can combine business with pleasure, can't we?"

"Don't know why not." She climbed into the car, and they drove to her house. Eric waited behind the wheel while she went to change. It wasn't until she pulled on her yellow swim suit that she realized what she had let herself in for. It would be the first time outside the rehab clinic that she had appeared in a swim suit, and she wasn't sure she was ready for it.

She stood before the full-length mirror on her closet door, studying her body, her leg. For an instant, it was like looking into a fun-house mirror that distorted shapes, but in the next instant, she knew she was seeing reality. She tried to tell herself that her injured leg was filling out, but in all honesty, she had to admit that it was at least a fourth smaller than her good leg. And her built-up shoe would be useless in the sea. She would limp.

What a bummer! Why had she agreed to go swimming with Eric? But it was too late to back out now. Maybe she could delay the swimming or even cancel it out later. She pulled her jeans over her swim suit, tugged on a shirt and grabbed a comb. When she faced Eric again, she smiled as if she had nothing on her mind more important than locating fishing spots on a chart.

They drove back to the marina, boarded the *Starfish* and left the marina basin for open water.

"Where to?" Eric asked. "Got any favorite spots?"

"Lots of them." She shaded her eyes with her hand as sun glinted on the lime-green water. How many colors the sea had! "Why don't we head toward the Marquesas? There are some good fishing spots down that way."

"Fine with me. You want to take the wheel?"

Kit shook her head. "You're doing fine. I'll show you where the channels are. You'll learn faster at the wheel."

They skimmed across gentle waves at a leisurely speed, passing sailboaters, lobster fishermen and snorkelers. It was almost noon before Kit saw the distant Marquesas islets pushing through the surface like mounding green cushions.

"Now where?" Eric asked as they came closer to the first island. "Can you put us in at a good swimming beach?"

Kit took the wheel and turned into a channel she had used many times. But that day there was already a boat pulled onto the sand and a group of kids was running up and down the beach. She turned the *Starfish* around and headed for another spot.

"Got aced out of that one, huh?" Eric asked.

"Yeah, but I know another place." She nosed the bow into another channel, and they soon reached a secluded cove where the water shimmered like white wine as it washed onto the shore. A cormorant perched on a gray coral rock protruding from the sea, his wings spread as if he enjoyed a sun bath. At their approach, he made a loud screech and flapped into the dense growth of mangrove trees that covered the island.

"Neat spot, Kit." Eric grinned as he looked at the uninhabited key, the sandy beach. "We could be the only two people on earth. Maybe everyone else has disappeared."

"Maybe, but I doubt it." She cut the motor and

dropped the anchor over the side. "Shall we wade to shore and have lunch?"

"Maybe we'd better swim first." Eric began skinning from his jeans and shirt. "If we eat first, we'll have to wait to swim."

"Okay." Still Kit didn't remove her jeans or shirt.

"Modest?" Eric teased. "I'll turn my back. No peeking. Promise."

Kit felt herself blushing, but she agreed. "Do that, Eric."

"If you don't mind, I'll just splash on to shore." The water was waist deep, and Eric held the lunch high, protecting it from the sea.

Kit removed her jeans and shirt, sat on the gunwale, then splashed into the clear warm water. At first, the turtle grass brushing against her ankles claimed her full attention. She always wondered just what creatures might be lurking in that grass, but as usual, nothing seemed to be present except grass. As she neared the shore, the water was only calf deep, not deep enough to hide her leg, and when she reached the sand where Eric waited, he was openly studying her legs. She walked on tiptoe to avoid limping.

"I was expecting to see a withered leg," Eric said frankly. "Withered. That's what my grandmother said. I'm glad she was wrong."

"You needn't try to make me feel better about it. I know how my leg looks and how it should look."

"It's smaller than your other leg, Kit. Sure it is, but it isn't withered. Not at all. And are you supposed to walk on tiptoe like that?"

"If I want to, I can. It keeps me from limping. And that's why I wear the special shoe—to make the limp less noticeable and to place less strain on my back. But each day I'm supposed to walk some without the shoe, to stretch those leg muscles and get them back in shape."

"Then now's a good time to do it," Eric said. "After we swim, of course. Race you to those rocks out there."

And the race was on. Suddenly, Kit felt totally at ease with Eric. He had looked at her leg quite frankly, and he hadn't died of shock. And she hadn't died of embarrassment. He had accepted her as she was, accepted her handicap more gracefully than she had imagined possible. She had been much harder on herself than Eric had been. Maybe that's the way it always was. Maybe nobody else noticed her leg as much as she did. And maybe nobody expected as much from her as she expected from herself.

She swam. She floated on her back. She dived. How easily her body glided through the water. Except for the brine stinging her eyes, she felt at home in the sea. They never decided who won the race to the rocks because Kit had stopped to float and to peer at the bottom. But Eric won the race back to shore.

"Good!" he cried. "The lunch is still here."

"Where did you think it would be?" Kit tucked her dripping hair behind her ears and felt brine trickle down her neck and back.

"Who knows? Maybe some old salt who has been shipwrecked for fifty years right on this island spied us and came to investigate our lunch."

"Well, we'll have to leave him some scraps when we leave." As they ate Maggie McGinnis's sandwiches, washing them down with Coke, Kit smiled at the way the sea water made Eric's hair curl even more tightly. When they finished eating, they stretched out on the sand and watched ragged cloud formations scud past them as the wind began to pick up. Kit closed her eyes, thinking how easy it would be to fall asleep, and when she opened them again, Eric had moved closer to her. Slowly and tenderly, he brushed his lips against hers, then moved away from her again. It happened so quickly that she wondered for a few seconds if she had imagined the kiss. But no. It had been real. Eric said nothing, and she suddenly felt very uneasy.

"Maybe we should start back, Eric. I wouldn't want to be caught out here in a squall. Storms can brew quickly in the summertime."

"I didn't mean to scare you away."

"You didn't scare me away." She looked directly at him. "Not at all."

"Then prove it by taking one more dip. I've brought a snorkel in the boat. I'd like to take a quick look under the surface."

"Okay, but let's make it short. The wind's really coming up." Kit sensed that they both were hiding their feelings behind superficial chatter about the sea and the wind. She felt suddenly shy, and she wondered if Eric felt that way, too.

They splashed to the boat, and Eric grabbed his mask and snorkel, then swam toward the rocks they had visited earlier.

"Do you dive?" Eric asked.

"I have scuba gear, but I've never used it in the sea. Only in the clinic pool." She shivered. The water seemed colder now.

Eric swam to the left of the rocks, face submerged, breathing through the snorkel tube. At last, he raised his head and swam toward her.

"Hey, come look, Kit. I've spotted a bunch of ballast stones."

"Ballast stones from what?"

"From an old galleon, probably."

"You're putting me on."

"Am not. I think that's exactly what they are. Come see."

Kit slipped on the face mask but refused the snorkel. "I can hold my breath long enough to look." She swam over the area where Eric had been and peered through the greenish water that she guessed might be twenty feet deep at that spot. At first, she could make out nothing unusual on the bottom. Then she saw the pile of stones that Eric had seen. It looked like a low heap of footballs. At least the stones were about the size of footballs. They were all bunched together except for a few that had scattered to one side. She lifted her head and removed the mask.

"How do you know those are ballast stones?"

"It's just an educated guess. Want me to bring one up?"

She glanced at the sky. "We'd better go, Eric. I smell a storm, and that water's very deep at this point."

"I can make it," Eric insisted. Before Kit could argue, he had donned the mask again, thrust the snorkel into her hand and disappeared beneath the surface.

9

Kit studied the surface, which had turned a dull gray-green color when clouds masked the sun, and she waited only a few seconds before she grabbed a deep breath, ducked under the waves and tried to find Eric. The salt water stung her eyes, and fear raised goose flesh on her arms and legs. Where was he?

A few more seconds passed before she spotted his form far below her, swimming gracefully around the heap of stones. Graceful. She felt graceful herself as the brine buoyed her body, giving her a sense of weightlessness. Since her injury, she felt much more agile in water than out of it. The water was like an invisible net, giving her a sense of security.

It seemed a long time, but she knew Eric had been on the bottom only a minute or so. Then he popped to the surface, carrying one of the encrusted stones under one arm. He gasped for air, flung the sea water from his eyes and treaded water.

"Here it is." He raised the stone for Kit's inspection.

She glanced at it and nodded. "Let's swim to the boat, Eric. We can examine the stone there. We need to head for home."

"Right." Eric looked at the clouds and shouted, "Race you!"

Was he kidding? How could he race and carry the stone at the same time! But he did. And his one-armed crawl brought him to the boat ahead of her.

"You're some swimmer," she said once she was seated on the bow facing Eric behind the wheel.

"Thought you'd never notice," he said as he started the motor and pointed the boat toward Key West.

Gray coral encrusted the oval-shaped stone in many places. "So you think this really came off an ancient ship?" Kit scraped at the coral with her fingernail.

"I'm almost sure of it. I've read about divers finding piles of stones like that one we saw. The stones were probably in the hold of a galleon. The ship sank. The timbers rotted away, leaving the stones in a heap on the sea bottom."

"But if the galleons were treasure ships, why would their captains have used space to carry stones? Were they trying to fool pirates? I mean did some galleons carry silver and gold and others carry worthless stones?"

"No. Every galleon was a treasure ship. They were unwieldy vessels, and they weren't built for speed. They were built for the temporary caching of wealth. Each ship had three or four decks, and each ship carried a lot of weight in masts and sails. It had to carry ballast to balance out all that upper weight."

"Still seems like a poor use of space." Kit felt the sun warming her shoulders. The threatening storm had fizzled out. She relaxed.

"I suppose the captain could offload some of the ballast if he took on cargo to replace it, but the captain had to account for every item aboard his ship."

"*Every* one?"

"Right. When the galleons set sail from Spain, they carried tools and manufactured goods to Spanish colonists in the New World. But on the return trip, the galleons carried items much in demand by the stay-at-home Spaniards." Eric slowed the *Starfish,* since the danger of a squall had passed.

Kit was glad they had slowed down. It would give her more time with Eric. She remembered his gentle kiss, but she kept her mind on his words. She was discovering more and more facets to Eric's personality. "What kinds of items did the galleons carry?"

"Oh, tobacco, emeralds, pearls, dyes. All those things came aboard in addition to the most important cargo—gold and silver. Spain's House of Trade required each galleon to carry a registry listing of every item aboard."

Kit looked across the water and then down at the ballast stone. "It's hard to believe we're cutting along the same route that a treasure ship might have sailed centuries ago. It's sort of, sort of *awesome,* isn't it?"

Eric grinned at her. "Better watch out. You're getting hooked."

"Hooked on what?"

"Hooked on the lore of ancient Spain."

Kit watched a gull circle the *Starfish,* then leave when it saw there were no fish aboard. "Anyone would find treasure stories fascinating. I'd like to know more about those galleons." Suddenly, it pleased her very much to be interested in the same thing Eric was interested in.

"I'd like to know more about them, too. That's why I want to study ancient Spanish history. At least it's one of the reasons."

"What will you do with a degree in that area? I mean what sort of a job will you get after you graduate?"

"Maybe a teaching job at a university. Maybe I could be a research person for historians. Or for treasure hunters. People who can read the ancient documents in the Spanish archives have a valuable source of information. A scholar working in Seville's Archive of the Indies helped Mel Fisher locate the artifacts from the *Atocha.* Dr. Lyon. I told you about him that day we met at the clinic."

"I'm impressed."

"According to my reading, the route of the galleons seldom varied. As they returned to Spain, they left Havana on a northward route until they saw the Florida keys. At that point, they would head east, sailing on the Gulf Stream. But they stuck close to the keys for as long as they could." Eric waved to a friend who sped by them on water skis.

"Surely the captains of the galleons knew that the shallow waters around the keys were dangerous."

"But they didn't have our modern compasses and radar to help them navigate," Eric said. "They liked to keep in sight of land. Even though they always sailed in convoy, they knew that at least ten percent of the galleons would go down."

"Ten percent!" Kit shuddered. "Think of all those lost lives! How could Spain survive so much tragedy?"

"You and I might think of lost lives, but Spanish officials thought mainly in terms of gold and silver. Most of the galleons leaving the New World were overloaded. Riches were more important than human life. Spain was greedy."

"Eric! We might be floating over lost treasure right this minute."

"Right." Eric grinned at her. "But the Spanish usually did everything in their power to salvage the sunken cargo."

"They sound like a bunch of crazies. First they overload their ships; then they try to salvage what was lost. Why didn't they just not overload in the first place?"

"I tell you, they were greedy. The House of Trade decreed the exact number of biscuits a ship could carry on a voyage that would last for months, but regulations were lax where gold and silver were concerned. If a galleon were lost, who could prove for sure that she had been overloaded. Usually, there were no survivors."

"If an overloaded ship arrived safely, I suppose the officials were too elated over the fresh riches to nitpick about cargo weight."

"You've got it, Kit. The bottom line was always money."

"I'd like to see the artifacts from the *Atocha* sometime," Kit said. "I've seen part of them, but now, after actually finding a ballast stone and after hearing all you've told me, I'd like to take a closer look at what Mel Fisher's divers have recovered."

"I'd like to show you through the exhibition, Kit. How about it? I can get us in for free."

Kit's heart thudded a bit faster at the thought of another outing with Eric. "How can you get us in free?" She delayed accepting the invitation, although she wanted to pounce on it. Had Eric forgotten about Dian? She hoped so. Surely visiting the *Atocha* exhibition couldn't be construed as a business trip.

"Henry has worked for Fisher, and some free passes to the exhibition came as a fringe benefit. How about it?"

"It'll be too late tonight."

"Then we'll go tomorrow. If we don't have a charter."

"I'll see. Let's wait and see how tomorrow shapes up businesswise." Why was she hesitating? Sometimes she didn't understand herself.

"Okay."

Now they were approaching Key West under blue skies and a few high clouds. Kit pulled her jeans over her swim suit, pleased that she had felt no special need to hide her weak leg on the return trip. It was nice to feel at ease with Eric, to know he wasn't being critical of her looks. She smiled to herself, thinking that it had been the first time she had really relaxed about her injury since the night of the accident. Eric had given her a lot to think about besides her leg. His kiss. His treasure stories. His plan to show her the *Atocha* treasure.

"What are you smiling about?" Eric asked.

She felt her smile grow broader. "Everything. It's been a good day—one of those good days everyone is always telling everyone else to have."

Eric guided the *Starfish* past Key West and on to Stock Island and the Coral Cove Marina. They secured the boat in its slot, picked up the debris from their lunch, then walked through the marina office, heading toward Eric's car. Before they reached the Ford, Kit stopped abruptly. Eric hadn't noticed yet, but Dian was sitting in his car in the passenger seat. Waiting. How long had she been there? Had Eric known she was going to be there?

"Eric, I just remembered, I have to make a phone call."

"Okay. I'll wait."

"No. You go on. Dad was going to come out here and we were going to choose some tackle for gramp for his birthday. You go on. I'll wait for dad and ride back to town with him."

"Okay, if you say so. But I'd better wait until you get him on the line. I wouldn't want to leave you stranded."

She tried to get Eric to leave, but he refused. He still hadn't noticed Dian. Kit went to the phone in the marina office and dialed her home. "Dad? Kit here."

Once Eric saw that she'd made the connection, he waved good-bye and walked on toward his car. Kit kept her father on the line until she was sure Eric was gone; then she waited outside the marina until her dad came to pick her up.

"What's up, Kit?" her father asked as he stopped the car. "You and Eric have a spat?"

"No. Nothing like that. It's just that Eric has this

girl friend, and I don't want to do anything to make her jealous of me. You know what I mean, don't you? I mean Eric and I have a business deal going, and I'd hate for anything to ruin it." She tried to believe her own words. They sounded logical, didn't they? She tried to forget Eric's kiss.

"Good idea to play it safe," her dad agreed. "But surely his girl friend knows he's working with you, doesn't she?"

"I don't know. Eric has only mentioned her name once, and then it was a very casual mention. And dad, we didn't take a customer out today. We had a no-show. We've just been out swimming and having fun. And his girl was waiting in his car when we got back."

"I wouldn't worry too much about it," her dad said. "Of course the girl might not understand Eric's spending his free time with you."

"In a way, it was business. We were marking down fishing areas on a chart for Eric so he can learn the waters around here." She felt twinges of guilt. They really hadn't spent all that much time marking fishing areas. They had spent a lot more time swimming and eating and talking about Spanish treasure.

Once at home, Kit helped with supper preparations and the cleanup afterward; then she went upstairs to soak in the tub and to rest. She was surprised later in the evening when the phone rang and it was for her.

"I think it's Eric," her mother said.

"Maybe we have a charter for tomorrow, mom. Maybe today's no-show got his dates mixed up. Maybe we're going to get to take him out, after all."

"Kit," Eric said. "I just called to see if you'd like

to visit the treasure exhibition with me tomorrow morning. I've checked the phone. No calls for tomorrow."

"Oh." Kit realized she sounded disappointed, and she tried to cover her lack of enthusiasm. She did want to go with him, didn't she? What did she want? A letter from Dian, saying it was okay for them to go out together? "I'd like to see the exhibition, Eric. Are you sure you have time to take me?"

The line hummed for a moment before he replied. "Of course I have the time. We don't have a charter for tomorrow. I just told you. No calls."

"Right. I thought that's what you might be calling to tell me, that we did have a charter."

"Sorry to disappoint you."

Why was she saying everything wrong? It was a wonder Eric didn't hang up on her. "I'd love to see the treasure, Eric. What time shall we go?"

"How about around ten o'clock? There shouldn't be much of a crowd then. Henry says most of the tourists show up in the afternoon. We'll probably have the place pretty much to ourselves."

"Fine. I'll be ready. I'll be looking forward to it." Had she sounded too eager? She seemed to be going from one extreme to another.

"See you, then. And by the way, I have an idea for using those ballast stones we found. I think we can make a good profit."

"How?"

"I'll tell you tomorrow. It could be a good deal for us. See you then."

"Yeah. See you, Eric."

She replaced the receiver, then stared at it for a few seconds. Had Eric Hartley just asked her for a real date for the next morning, a date to see the treasure? Or was it another business meeting? If he had financial plans for the ballast stones, then maybe his mind was strictly on business. But of course it must be. The day before, when he had left the marina with Dian, he had been smiling at her, talking to her as if he were really glad to see her.

Kit did her exercises, and again she retired early, tired from the day on and in the water. She wondered if she would ever get her full strength back. Before the accident, she had been able to stay up late at night and get up early in the morning. She had seldom felt tired. But now, even with vitamins and lots of extra rest, she still felt dragged out early in the evening.

The next morning, a glance at the calendar told her that in three days the teen tournament would end. She regretted being unable to try to fish, and she wondered if Eric had gone out for black-tip during their free days. She knew she couldn't bear to ask. And she also knew that he would never volunteer the information. For all she knew, he might have surpassed her record. Could she handle that?

Eric came to the door around ten o'clock, and they drove the few blocks to the treasure museum. Eric smiled and flashed passes at the gatekeeper as they walked inside the red brick building. Kit felt uneasy at the sight of an armed guard near the entrance, but she supposed a guard was essential. The artifacts in the building were priceless. She felt even more uneasy when she saw Dian poring over some charts near a coin exhibit. She stiffened, wishing she could leave the building immediately. Why had Eric brought her here?

"What's the matter?" Eric grinned. "I guess the sight of this stuff is overwhelming the first time you see it all together. Come on; I want you to meet Dian. She works here, and she'll show us around."

Eric led the way to the glass-enclosed case where Dian was making notes in a book. She looked up at their approach, and Kit was surprised to see that she looked quite a bit older than Eric. It was hard to guess her age, but she looked old enough to be in her twenties. Of course, Eric was eighteen. He was out of high school. Maybe he liked older women. Kit forced a smile, and Dian smiled back.

"Kit, I'd like for you to meet Dian. . . ."

Someone dropped a carton of books just as Eric said Dian's last name, and Kit didn't hear it distinctly. And she felt too ill at ease to ask for a repeat. At least Dian seemed friendly. And she didn't seem to mind that Eric had brought her to view the treasure.

"Kit's the girl I've been telling you about, Dian," Eric said. "The one I'm working with on the charter-boat trips."

"I'm glad to meet you, Kit," Dian said. "Eric says you're interested in seeing some Spanish artifacts."

"Yes, I am," Kit said.

"Dian's a marine archaeologist," Eric said. "She's helped pinpoint on charts exactly where lots of these artifacts were found."

"A marine archaeologist?" Kit asked.

"Yes." Dian answered her smoothly and coolly. "I have my degree from Miami University, and I've gained lots of experience from working on the *Atocha* artifacts."

"Working underwater?" Kit asked. "Diving?"

"Some of the work was underwater," Dian said.

"And lots of it is done above the water, the cataloging of the artifacts and details like that. Many treasure hunters snatch up artifacts thinking only of their monetary value. Such treasures are almost valueless to historians."

"But much of the *Atocha* treasure has been cataloged," Eric said. "It can be studied by students and historians in years to come. The *Atocha* treasure is valuable in many ways."

Dian led them to an exhibit of gold bars; she brought one out of the case and laid it in Kit's hand. Kit felt goose bumps rise on her arm as she hefted the cold weight of the treasure bar.

"How can you risk letting people hold this treasure?" she asked. "Aren't you afraid someone will try to steal it?"

"We do have some guards to help prevent theft," Dian said with a laugh. "But Mr. Fisher likes to see people actually hold pieces of the treasure. He wants them to have the experience of feeling Spanish gold." Dian pointed out the indentations on the gold bar in Kit's hand. "On one side, you see the cross of Christianity, but on the other side you see the mark of the conquistadors. The gold is as two-faced as Spain herself was in those days, the mark of Christ alongside the mark of men who plundered the New World under the flag of Spain."

Kit returned the gold bar to Dian, who laid it back in the display case. The feel of Spanish gold. Kit thought she would never forget the experience. It had stretched her mind in a way that would never allow it to return to its former shape. She wanted to know more about Florida and Spain and about herself in relationship to them.

"Come on," Eric said. "I'll show you lots more stuff. We'll be here all day if we don't get a move on."

Kit followed him to display cases of silver coins. Some of them were brightly polished, and others lay in clumps encrusted together by coral.

"The silver coins all had to be cleaned," Eric explained. "The average person could see a silver coin washed up on the beach and never realize what he was looking at. Not so with gold coins."

Eric guided Kit to a case containing gold doubloons. "See? The ocean does nothing to disfigure gold. It's as bright as the day it was lost."

Kit followed Eric through the museum, viewing anchors, money chains, ruby-set rosaries, Spanish muskets, silverware, navigation instruments. She tried to imagine life aboard a treasure galleon, the months spent in crossing the ocean to the New World, then returning to Spain. And she couldn't help thinking of those who had never returned. The whole *Atocha* exhibition was a monument to tragedy; at the same time, it was a historian's look into the past, an adventurer's dream come true. She couldn't sort out her feelings, but she was beginning to realize that the sea hid many things other than fish.

They wandered through the exhibits until more people began to arrive and the aisles and pathways became crowded.

"Ready to go?" Eric asked.

"I guess so. But a person could stay in here for hours and still not see everything on display."

"Right. But we can come back another time if you're really interested."

As they started to leave, Kit didn't know whether or not she should say something more to Dian; maybe thank her again for allowing her to hold the gold bar. But as they strolled back toward the exhibit where Dian was working, other visitors were crowding around her, making it hard for them to get her attention.

"I'd like to tell her thanks," Kit said.

"She's busy now. I'll give her your message later."

Kit felt a quick intake of breath almost choke her. Eric made no pretense of not seeing Dian frequently. She wanted to ask him how he happened to be going out with an older girl. But it really was none of her business. None at all. Eric looked mature for his age. He didn't have that unfinished look so many boys had. He could pass for twenty. Maybe even older, she guessed. And she also guessed that Dian wouldn't feel out of place being seen with Eric. Not at all.

"I've been saving the good news for last," Eric said as he stopped in front of Kit's house again.

"What? We've got another charter?" She looked at him eagerly.

"You must be psychic. We do have another charter. This guy called early this morning. A Mr. Relding. He's booked for a half day tomorrow, and I made a special trip to the marina to meet him and to collect a deposit fee."

"Good deal, Eric! He'll surely show up. A guy's not apt to forfeit money by being a no-show."

Eric nodded, but he wasn't smiling, and Kit sensed his apprehension. "What's the matter?"

"Oh, nothing. Nothing really. It's just that I didn't warm up to this guy."

"Why not?"

"Nothing I could put my finger on. He just seemed like the kind who might really pitch a fit if he didn't make a catch."

"We'll see to it that he catches something. We'll convince him that 'cuda on the flats can be fun. Surely we'll be able to stand him for a half day."

"I suppose."

Eric didn't sound as sure of himself as he usually did, and Kit wondered about this Mr. Relding. What if he gave them a bad time the next day? What if he bad-mouthed their operation when he got back from his trip? They didn't need that kind of publicity.

10

After Eric took her home, Kit spent the rest of the day resting, exercising and washing the downstairs windows as a surprise for her parents. But all the time she was working, she was thinking about Mr. Relding, about the negative impression he had made on Eric. She tried to visualize the problems they might encounter with such a customer, and as she drew mental images of Mr. Relding's probable reactions to happenings on the flats, she considered tactful words to counteract them. She had learned that she usually handled a situation to the best of her ability if she had taken the time to mentally picture what she might logically expect to happen. Practicing the future—that's what her dad called it. But he never laughed at her, and many times the practicing paid off.

The next morning, she dressed in fresh chinos, a

brown tank top that matched her hair and a tan cotton shirt that she could either wear or lay aside. Neat enough, she thought as she viewed the effect in the mirror. Businesslike, if your business was fishing. Nothing there a customer could complain about. She knew Eric would look fresh and clean. He always did. Sometimes people used the sea and sun as excuses for a sloppy appearance, but Kit had found that it was just as easy to look neat as it was to look grungy.

"All set?" Eric asked as she scooted onto the car seat beside him.

"As all set as I'll ever be. Maybe you misread this guy's signals, Eric."

"You been worrying about him?"

"A little. But maybe he's mellowed a bit during the night."

"Like a green avocado in a dark drawer?" Eric laughed. "I hope so. But let's don't worry about him until we have to. I didn't mean to get you bent out of shape over him."

"I'm not bent out of shape. I'm just sort of uneasy."

"I've got good news about the ballast stones. That should take your mind off your uneasiness."

"Give. I'd almost forgotten you said you had an idea about using them."

"I was talking with my brother and with Dian at dinner night before last, and they think we should stop by the Rusty Anchor and talk to the owner about the stones."

At dinner. With Dian at dinner. The words dinned in her ears. He had taken Dian to dinner. Or maybe he had invited her to eat at his house. More likely, that was what happened. Henry had been there, too. She wondered what kind of a dinner they had had. Did Eric cook? Or maybe Henry did the cooking. Or maybe he had invited Dian because she would cook for them. Maybe she should learn to cook something and invite Eric over to her house for dinner. She would talk to her mother about it. Soon.

"What do you think, Kit? I mean if you don't like the idea of diving for the stones, trying to sell them, well, we don't have to do it. Or maybe I could do it on my own. But since we found them together, I thought you might want to make them another of our business ventures."

Kit pulled her thoughts back to the matter at hand. Her speechlessness over hearing him mention Dian's name so casually had given him the wrong impression. "*Sell* the stones? What makes you think anyone would buy them? Oh, I know they're interesting and all that, but anyone who wants them could go out and get them."

"Not anyone," Eric said. "A person has to know exactly where they are."

"True."

"And a person has to know how to swim and how to dive."

"Again, true."

"Didn't you tell me you owned scuba gear? That would help. We could both dive in our scuba gear, and it wouldn't take long to bring the stones to the surface."

"But why would the owner of the Rusty Anchor be interested in buying them?"

Henry thought we should ask. Greg White. That's his name. He's just opened that café, and Henry said

Mr. White asked him about buying some salvage items for outdoor landscaping. Henry sold him a big anchor, and Henry thinks Greg might like to use the ballast stones as ground cover around the anchor. I think it would make a neat decoration. What do you think?"

"We can go talk to him, sure. I've never tried my scuba gear in the sea; only in the clinic pool. I'm not sure I'd be much help in bringing up the stones."

"Water's water." Eric laughed. "No reason your gear won't work in the sea. I'm glad you're a strong swimmer. It's going to take some muscle to move all those stones."

"Are you sure it's legal to take them, Eric? I mean, would we be stealing?"

"It's legal to take them," he assured her. "The Marquesas island area is far enough from the Florida mainland that the state would have no jurisdiction over our find. I promised to chart the spot on a map for Dian. She's going to lend me her underwater camera so I can take some photos of the stones before we move them. That way she'll have exact information on where they were found just in case such information should ever be valuable historically."

"An underwater camera! She's a photographer, too?"

"Yes." Eric nodded. "Underwater photography is a necessary activity for a marine archaeologist. I've used Dian's camera before, and I've had fair luck with it. No problem there."

Kit felt very much the nobody as she compared herself to Dian. No wonder Eric liked her. She was pretty. No, that was an understatement. She was beautiful. She was a professional archaeologist. She could dive. She could take underwater pictures. And she had showed Eric how to use her camera. Kit sighed.

"What's wrong? Tired before we even get started?"

"No. I was just thinking about all the things Dian can do and how few I can do."

Eric laughed and shook his head. "I try never to make comparisons. At least not *that* kind of comparison. I just try to compare myself to myself."

"I don't get it. What do you mean?"

"If I do some special thing that interests me, then I try to do it better the next time. I try to improve my own record. To me, that's the only kind of comparison that makes any sense."

Was Eric just trying to make her feel better about having so little going for her? She didn't want him feeling sorry for her. No way. She still held the black-tip record, didn't she! Well, at least she hoped she did. Surely, if Eric had bettered her record, he would have said so. She guessed that Dian might not know anything about fishing, especially not about fishing for black-tip.

"Here we are," Eric said, leaving the car in his usual spot. "Let's hope for the best."

They walked through the cool marina office and out to the dock where they readied the *Starfish* for a day on the water. There wasn't much to do, since they had cleaned it well the last time they used it. Eric filled the gasoline tank, then tested the motors and the radio. And they waited.

"Maybe he won't show up," Kit said. "Maybe he's so rich he won't mind losing his deposit."

"Wishful thinking." Eric nodded toward a large burgundy-colored Lincoln just pulling into the parking lot. "There he is, Kit. I knew he'd show."

Kit eyed the short, stout man, fortyish, dressed in white slacks and sport shirt and wearing a navy blue skipper's cap. She was glad the *Starfish* was spotlessly clean and that they were neatly dressed. Their appearance gave her confidence.

"Good morning, mates," Mr. Relding said in a roaring, high-tide voice. "Are we ready to cast off?"

"Right, sir." Eric led the way through the marina office and to the dock. "You may sit in the fishing chair, sir. I think you'll find it comfortable."

"I prefer to stand on the poling platform," Mr. Relding said. "I can see better from up there. The fishing chair places me too close to the water for a good overview of the flats."

Eric hesitated, looking at Kit, who took his look as her cue to speak. This is a problem she hadn't anticipated. "Mr. Relding, we're sorry, but when the boat is in transit to the fishing grounds, everyone must be seated. It's a rule designed for your safety as well as ours."

"Who are you?" Mr. Relding demanded, looking at Kit sharply. "Thought Captain Hartley was in charge of this boat. He's certainly the person I made arrangements with."

"Captain Hartley is in charge," Kit agreed, forcing a customer-is-always-right smile.

"Then let's let Captain Hartley make the rules, shall we?" Mr. Relding looked expectantly at Eric.

Eric cleared his throat and looked at a spot just to the left of Mr. Relding's right eye. "Kit is my partner, Mr. Relding, and she is right about the safety rules. Everyone remains seated until we reach the fishing grounds."

Mr. Relding muttered, but he took his place in the fishing chair, dropping a heavy canvas bag beside him.

And that was the beginning of their rotten morning. Kit couldn't believe a morning could be so bad. When it came to complaining, Mr. Relding was a ten. And he drank beer all the way to the fishing flats. By the time they reached the backwaters, he could hardly keep his balance as he stood on the bow of the boat trying to spot fish. At last, he splashed into the water, rod in one hand, bowline in the other, and he pulled the boat through the thigh-deep shallows.

"Sir," Kit said. "It's dangerous for you to be in the water. There are sharks on these flats. And rays. And barracuda."

Before she could continue, a churning of the water at Mr. Relding's feet startled them, and they watched a huge ray shoot across the flats, leaving a trail of mud behind him. Kit knew that would have scared every fish in the area back into deep water, but she said nothing. She and Eric both remained silent while Mr. Relding towed them across the flats in spite of her warning.

They saw but one fish the whole morning, and by the time Mr. Relding got ready to cast, the fish had disappeared. At eleven-thirty Eric spoke.

"If you'll get back in the boat, sir, it's time for us to be heading back to the marina."

"Don't want to go back." Mr. Relding glared at Eric. "I've decided to stay the whole day."

"But you only signed up for a half day," Eric said.

Mr. Relding reached into his pocket, pulled out a roll of bills and began peeling off twenties. "Guess this will pay for the other half day."

Eric looked at Kit, and she shook her head. He winked to acknowledge his agreement with her decision. "I'm sorry, Mr. Relding, but we have plans for the afternoon. If you'll please get into the boat, we'll head back now."

"What's the matter with you, boy? Can't you see I'm offering you good money? You'll stay out here as long as I care to stay and pay."

"No, sir," Eric replied. "We won't do that at all. I'm taking the *Starfish* in right now. If you care to ride along, you're welcome. You've paid for the trip. But if you want to remain here, that's fine, too. We'll arrange for someone at the marina to come pick you up at any time you choose."

"Leave me out here alone!" Mr. Relding's face grew crimson. "You'll do no such thing." He boarded the boat immediately, and Kit lost no time in opening the motor and heading for the marina. Once they were at the dock, Mr. Relding went raging into the Coral Cove office, and Kit rested her head on the steering wheel of the boat, completely disheartened.

"Hey, kids," a man called from the gasoline pumps. "Don't let old Relding get you down."

Kit lifted her head. "But he's going to ruin our business, our reputation."

"No, he isn't," the man said. "Everyone around here knows him. Nobody pays him any mind. Everyone will give you two lots of respect for turning down his money. He offered you cash to stay out longer, didn't he?"

"How did you know?" Kit asked.

"Just a sharp guess," the man said. "Relding has a habit of booking a boat for a half day. If he catches, then he comes in at noon. But if he doesn't catch, then he offers more money for a full day."

"It didn't work with us," Eric said.

"Wise decision on your part." The man chuckled. "You've just graduated from semipros to full professionals."

Kit and Eric exchanged brief glances; then they hosed the boat and headed for Eric's car.

"What a day!" Eric said.

"Hope that man's right about Mr. Relding," Kit said. "I sort of hated to turn down the money."

"Yeah, I know what you mean. We may need money, but we don't need it that much, Kit. What do you say we stop at the Rusty Anchor right now and talk to Greg White about the ballast stones?"

"Fine with me." Kit leaned her head back against the seat cushion, relaxing for the first time that day. This time she wasn't surprised when Eric took her hand, but she wasn't sure of his motivations. Did he like her? Or was he trying to comfort her after a bad day on the sea? Did he put Dian out of his thoughts when he held another girl's hand? She wished she wouldn't ask herself so many questions. Sometimes the thing to do was to accept what came and enjoy.

The Rusty Anchor was located near the airport, and it was doing a big lunch business. Kit liked the weathered shake-shingle exterior and the brass-bound windows that had the look of portholes. And once inside the café, the sandwich bar attracted her immediately. The bar was fashioned into a long aquarium that ran the full length of the snack area.

Lights illumined the water, and the plate-glass sides and top of the bar allowed diners to watch a fascinating salt-water scene.

"What'll you have, kids?" A short wiry man who Kit guessed to be in his thirties swabbed a cloth over the glass in front of them and waited to take their orders. He wore a white sailcloth apron over his blue sport shirt and slacks, and his horn-rimmed glasses gave him an owlish look.

"Are you Greg White?" Eric asked.

"Right," the man answered. "Have we met before? Can't recall your name."

"You know my brother, Henry Hartley," Eric said. "He sent Kit and me here to talk over a business matter with you. But we'll do it over burgers and fries if that's okay."

"Kit?" Greg asked.

"Kit Cummings," Eric said. "We operate a charter boat out of Coral Cove Marina."

"Nice to meet you, Kit." Greg smiled at her; then he called their burger and fry order to a cook in the kitchen before he noted Kit's interest in the aquarium. "Like what you see down there, Kit?"

"It's beautiful," Kit replied, looking at a sand bottom studded with an assortment of shells and water plants. I've never seen an aquarium built into a snack bar before."

Greg White beamed his pleasure at her comment. "I've been a shell collector all my life. This aquarium lets me share my hobby with others. Know anything about shells?"

"Not much," Kit admitted.

"Me, either," Eric said as Greg looked at him

questioningly. "But they really are pretty, and so are the fish swimming among them."

"Got some plain shells and some fancy ones here," Greg began, pointing out specimens embedded in the sand, reeling off their scientific names along with their popular names. "That reddish one at your left is a Lion's Paw, and the grayish one just below it is a Kitten's Paw. Then right over here's a good specimen of a volute. Think that's my favorite of them all."

"Hey, man!" a voice shouted. "How about some service? We can't eat shells."

"The man's hungry," Eric said, smiling. "Don't let us keep you from your business."

Greg excused himself, waited on his customer, then returned to them, bringing along their burgers and fries. "You want to know about shells, you've come to the right place. I've got specimens of chitons, tooth shells, clams, snails and cephalopods."

"I believe you," Eric said. "I won't make you prove it."

"You got shells you can't identify, you bring them around and I'll help you out."

Another customer demanded service, and again Greg left them to wait on trade.

"Some guy," Kit said. "Really excited over shells. I'd like to know more about some of the fish he's got in there with all the shells."

"Ask and I'm sure he'll tell you all about them." Eric laughed. "Of course, we may be here all night if you ask, but don't let that stop you. I could get interested, too."

When Greg returned, Kit refrained from asking

about the fish in the aquarium, although she was curious. Did they grow to full-size fish? Or did they remain small? Maybe they were already full-sized. What were their names? Where had he found them? Here was another aspect of the sea that she hadn't thought much about before right this minute, yet she had loved the sea all her life. It gave her a strange feeling to realize how much she had missed out on.

"Now what was this deal your brother sent you here to talk about?" Greg asked Eric.

"We found some ballast stones we thought you might be interested in buying."

"Got them with you?"

"No. But we can get them quickly enough if you're interested in them."

"Where are they?"

"In the sea, man. In the sea."

"That covers a lot of territory."

"You're right. It does. But we know where they are, and we can find them again." Eric pulled a rough sketch from his shirt pocket. "My brother drew this sketch, Greg. Henry thought you might be interested in those stones, and this is how he thought you might use them as ground cover to point up your main artifact, the anchor. What do you think?"

Kit craned her neck to see the sketch, although it was upside down to her.

Greg White studied the sketch for some time, nodding and thinking and nodding some more. "Where are the stones, kids?"

"Sorry," Eric said. "That's our secret. You want them, we'll get them for you, for a price."

"What price?"

"Henry suggested two bucks each."

Kit held her breath, waiting to hear what Greg would say. There were a lot of stones down there. They represented a lot of money if this man really wanted to buy them.

"Two bucks each sounds reasonable," Greg said at last. "How many can you bring me? I'd want enough to make a good showing around the base of the anchor. I want enough so that people will notice them and perhaps ask some questions."

"Ask questions?" Kit asked.

"Sure. I'm looking for a conversation piece. I want people to ask about the anchor, the stones, then tell their friends about this neat thing Greg White's set up out at the Rusty Anchor. How many stones can you bring me?"

"Can you estimate how many you think you'll want?" Eric asked.

"A couple hundred? Got that many?"

"I think so," Eric said. "But I'm not sure. And we'll probably have to make more than one trip to bring that many in."

"Why don't you take a look at the stone we have in the car?" Kit suggested.

"Didn't know you had one with you," Greg said. "Show it to me. But finish your meal first. Plenty time to take a look after you're through eating."

Kit and Eric lingered over their sandwiches. Kit left the aquarium rather reluctantly, trying to see all the shells as she strolled toward the entry. Once they were outside, Eric opened the car trunk and brought out the ballast stone for Greg's inspection. Kit watched Greg's face, trying to guess his reaction. It had surprised her that he had seemed willing to buy the stones sight unseen. She hoped he wasn't going to change his mind.

"Good enough!" Greg replied as he hefted the stone from one hand to the other. Then he carried it to the base of the anchor positioned near the entry and stood back to study the effect. He walked from one side of the anchor to the other, and Kit knew he was trying to picture the whole area beneath the anchor covered with ballast stones.

"Okay, you two. It's a deal. You bring me two hundred of these stones and you've got yourself four hundred big ones. Want to see it in writing?"

"A handshake will do," Eric said. "We'll bring some of the stones in this afternoon."

"I'll be expecting you." Greg gave Eric a slap on the shoulder before he returned to his café.

"It's okay with you if we go diving this afternoon, isn't it, Kit?" Eric asked. "I should have checked with you, but I was eager to close the deal."

"I don't blame you," Kit said. "Let's get going."

"We've got our work cut out for us, Kit. Think you're up to it?" Greg's face clouded with concern.

"I'm as up to it as you are. Let's get our gear. You got air?"

"Right. And you?"

"Yes. A full tank." Kit said no more, not wanting Greg to know how uneasy she really felt about diving in the scuba gear. Would it really work in the sea in the same way it had worked for her in the pool?

They stopped by their homes to pick up their scuba equipment, then drove back to the marina, loaded the gear into the stern of the *Starfish* and headed toward the Marquesas. The sky was cloudless, and the sun was like liquid heat on their heads and shoulders.

Kit wore her suit under her clothes, but she kept her chinos and shirt on to protect her skin from an overdose of sun rather than because she was reluctant to expose her leg. It was good, absolutely great, to be able to relax and be herself.

"There are a lot of things to learn about the sea, aren't there?" Kit asked as Eric slowed the boat near the rocks where they had spotted the ballast stones.

"Lots and then some." Eric picked up the underwater camera he had brought along. "What did you have in mind?"

Kit wanted to ask how he happened to have Dian's camera at his house, but she didn't. They had been talking about the mysteries of the sea, and she held to the subject. "You'll think I'm nuts, but I was thinking about all the turtle grass on the flats. There must be tons and tons of it. Maybe someday someone will discover a use for it. Maybe someone will find a way to make it edible." Suddenly, she felt that she was making a fool of herself. She wanted Eric to like her, respect her, not laugh at her.

"What made you think about the turtle grass?" Eric asked, looking at her but not laughing at her idea.

She relaxed a bit. Why was she so up-tight? "Well, the Japanese eat some kinds of seaweed, don't they? Maybe this is seaweed that nobody has discovered yet as a food."

"Could be, I suppose, but I think I'll stick to burgers and fries if you don't mind." With camera in hand and face mask in place, Eric plunged overboard and swam on the surface until he spotted the ballast stones once more. Then he lifted his head.

"Here they are, Kit. Right here. I'm going to free dive and snap some pics for Dian."

Dian! What did Dian have that she didn't have? What made Dian so attractive to him? Her blond beauty, of course. Kit knew her own looks were quite ordinary. She tried to tell herself Eric's interest in Dian went deeper than physical appearance. Dian loved the sea. But she loved the sea, too. Surely Eric knew that by now. Didn't he feel anything special for her? She tried to tell herself that he did. He had held her hand. He had kissed her. But he had also kept a lot of safe distance between them, too.

She had some very special feelings for Eric, and she was tired of suppressing them, tired of hiding them behind their business relationship. Maybe she was even falling in love with Eric. She put that thought aside as she realized how long Eric had been beneath the surface. Maybe he was in trouble. Just as she prepared to dive to look for him, he surfaced.

"Got three photos," he called as he swam toward the boat. "That should be enough."

Kit hid her feelings of near panic. Using the boarding ladder, Eric climbed back into the boat; then he and Kit took turns helping each other into their scuba gear. Masks. Air tanks. Flippers. Kit was very conscious of the accidental touching of his fingers against her arms and her back as he adjusted her air tank.

"Sure you can manage?" he asked before he secured his mouthpiece.

"Stick near me," Kit said. "I don't think I'll have

any problems, but I wouldn't want to be down there alone."

"I'll be right there. Want me to go first, or do you want to go first?"

"Let's go over together," Kit suggested. They secured their mouthpieces, then let themselves splash backward over the gunwale and into the sea.

Kit felt the cool water envelop her, then inhaled deeply, smelling the rubbery scent of the breathing apparatus. She peered through her face mask at the underwater scene. It was like looking through a Seven-Up bottle. Everything looked a clear crystalline green. She swam just a few feet below the surface until she felt sure of herself; then she followed Eric, who had gone straight to the bottom and was hovering over the pile of ballast stones as he looked up at her.

Kit put aside her personal feelings about Eric, which had all but overwhelmed her a few minutes before, and now she kept her thoughts strictly on the business at hand. Ballast stones. There were so many of them.

As she joined him, he pointed to the rock formation at their right that they had sat on during their previous visit to the area. They swam toward the rocks, gazing at intricate formations of staghorn coral, at undulating sea fans, at a school of bright yellow fingerlings that looked as though they might have escaped from Greg Miller's aquarium. She wanted to talk to Eric, but of course she couldn't. She wanted to exclaim over all the underwater beauty that she had not known existed. The clinic pool was a far cry from this natural sea setting.

They swam around the rocks for a few more

minutes; then Eric motioned her back to the business of the day, the ballast pile. She joined him over the center of the heap of stones. Eric picked up one of the smaller specimens and handed it to her, placing it under her left arm, pointing up toward the boat. Kit started up, thrusting with her legs, trying not to think of all the trips they would have to make between the ballast pile and the boat before they had all the stones Greg White wanted. Two hundred stones. A hundred dives each. Could she face that? She doubted it, but she hated to tell Eric. No doubt Dian would have thought nothing of a hundred dives. She felt herself scowl. Why was she comparing herself to Dian!

When she reached the surface, she clung to the boat ladder and waited for Eric. He surfaced seconds after she did, placed his stone in the boat and turned to take hers. Then he removed his mouthpiece long enough to talk over a plan.

"Let's use the landing net, Kit."

"How do you mean?"

"We can dive together, fill the net with three or four stones, whatever it will hold, and bring them up, with each of us holding one side of the net."

"Hey, I think that'll work!" She felt an inner relief that she didn't tell him about. "It'll save us a lot of time, but do you think the mesh of the landing net is strong enough to hold those heavy stones?"

"It's held a lot of heavy fish. It's sturdy. And we'll take care not to overload it."

Eric climbed into the boat, and Kit watched the way the sea water sluiced from his body, the way the sun glinted on the golden bronze of his skin. He opened a portside compartment, removed the landing net and splashed into the water again. This time, he reached for her hand as they submerged, and Kit felt its warmth as the cool sea played against her skin. Heaven. She could spend the rest of her life diving with Eric. She wondered what he was thinking. Was his mind strictly on ballast stones and the sale of them to Greg White?

They were able to bring up three stones on the first dive with the net and four stones the second time. After they had boated about forty stones, Kit was beginning to feel very tired, and she signaled to Eric that she was ready to rest. Eric signaled that he wanted to make one more trip. He pointed to her and then to the boat, indicating that he wanted her to wait for him, but she shook her head. She went down with him. Again, they swam to the depths. Kit was so fascinated with the gradual change in the water temperature—cool, cold, colder, very cold—that she didn't notice the overhead shadow at first. And when she did notice it, she realized on second glance that it wasn't a shadow at all. A huge shark was cruising near the surface, cruising and circling and dropping lower and lower, closer and closer to where she and Eric were swimming.

11

Neither Kit nor Eric was prepared for the swirling rush of water that washed them against the pile of ballast stones in spite of their best efforts to control their movements, their location. In the next instant, Kit saw the silvery flash of a barracuda, and she knew immediately what was happening. The 'cuda had attracted the shark. A hammerhead. A scream seemed to pound through her pulse beat, yet all was deathly silent. Eric had released her hand, but now he reached for it again, and she clung to him, wondering what they could do to save themselves.

She tried to recall everything she had ever read about sharks and shark attacks and the victims' chances of escaping unharmed. Was it possible that the hammerhead hadn't seen them? Sharks had poor vision. She knew that from her fishing experiences.

Maybe this fellow hadn't seen them at all and was strictly interested in the barracuda.

How big was the hammerhead? As Eric pulled her behind him to the far side of the ballast pile, Kit tried to estimate the size of the shark. Eight feet? Ten feet? Now it was swimming closer, dangerously closer, lashing the water with its great tail. She stared at the gray-green body, the pale underbelly, the evil-looking crossbar on the head with eyes on the extreme ends. To Kit, the words hammerhead and danger were synonymous. But even in her fear she wondered how the creature could see. If one eye was seeing things on its right side and the other eye was seeing things on its left side, how could it know exactly what to focus on?

But focusing on its prey did not seem to be one of the shark's major problems. It had no trouble capturing the 'cuda. Kit saw half of the smaller fish disappear as the hammerhead's huge jaws closed on it. Now a reddish tinge of blood clouded the water. Kit knew that although sharks couldn't see very well, they had an acutely keen sense of smell. The mangled 'cuda was bad news. The scent of blood could attract other sharks from a wide area.

Eric tugged on her hand and pointed toward the surface. Kit nodded. The hammerhead was swimming in a large circle around them. Again, she held the hope that it hadn't seen them, that it had been intent on the 'cuda. But just as she and Eric were about to shove for the surface, it turned suddenly, its left eye glaring at them.

But did it really see them? Kit tugged on Eric's hand and hunkered down on the ballast stones. Maybe the shark would overlook them if they didn't move. Maybe it would leave the area. Those eyes. Those crazy eyes! She tried to focus her whole attention on the shark, but her mind flashed back to a time in third grade, to a teacher who the kids said had eyes in the back of her head. That teacher seemed to know what was going on in her classroom even when she had her back turned to the students. Old Hammerhead, they had nicknamed her. But why was she thinking of the past at a time like this? Their very lives were in danger. She forced herself to focus her complete attention on the shark.

Again, Eric tugged on her hand and pointed upward. The hammerhead had passed by them, and its back was toward them. It nosed the bottom, snarfed up the remaining half of the barracuda and swam on. Now was their chance—if they had a chance. They crouched for an instant, again preparing to shove off, but in that instant, the shark turned and zeroed in for an attack. Now there was no doubt as to its intent. When it was only a few feet from them, Eric grabbed a ballast stone, heaved it and hit the shark's nose. Kit grabbed another stone and flung it at the creature, striking it on the side. She knew her shot hadn't harmed the shark. Instead, it had only served to anger it.

The water was a gray swirl, the color of terror, as the great tail lashed again and the shark turned, making another pass at them. A fin scraped Kit's thigh like a saw with well-honed teeth. Eric shoved her behind him, pushing her down against the ballast stones. He released her hand as he took a batter's grip on the oak handle of the landing net. When the hammerhead made its next turn, its next attack, Eric struck the left side of its head with a direct blow of the handle, and he scored a second time with a well-aimed kick.

But what could a human do against this monster! Kit thought in that moment that they were going to die. The ballast pile offered too little protection, and Eric and a landing net were no match for this giant. Its tail lashed again, and it turned sharply. Kit grabbed another ballast stone, determined to fight to the end of her strength. But before she had a chance to fling the stone, a sea bass swam close enough to the shark to attract its attention. Once the bass realized its danger, it flashed away, darting for safety. The shark lost no time in giving chase.

Eric tugged on Kit's hand once more, and this time they didn't hesitate. They shoved toward the surface, kicking frantically with their flippers, slicing through the brine as quickly as they could. They surfaced a few feet from the boat and swam to it; then Eric hung back while Kit climbed the boarding ladder. Once she was aboard, she turned to offer him a hand. Her heart was pounding, and she half expected to see the shark's jaws break the surface. But that didn't happen, and in seconds they were both safely aboard the *Starfish*.

For a few minutes, they just sat with their backs propped against the side of the boat. Then Kit removed her face mask and her fins, and Eric did likewise. They helped each other from their air tanks. Then they just stood looking at each other, unable to speak, barely able to breathe. The sun was blazing down on them, but Kit was shivering, and goose flesh roughed the skin on her arms and legs. She reached for her shirt and wiped her face and hair. She didn't realize she was crying until Eric mentioned it.

"No sense in crying now, Kit. We're safe. We're okay. The shark's gone."

"I'm not crying." She wrapped her arms around her knees, trying to warm herself. She felt as if she might never know the comfort of being warm again.

Eric edged toward her and held her damp shirt for her. "Here, Kit. Put this on. You're shivering."

She slipped the shirt on over her wet swim suit, then reached for her jeans and tugged them on. Eric handed her her deck shoes, and she rammed her feet into them. She could feel tears on her cheeks, but she could do nothing to stop them. What was the matter with her? She knew they were safe. Yet she felt suspended, as if some unseen hand might drop her back into the sea.

They were still sitting on the bottom of the boat when Eric scooted closer to her and put an arm around her as he wiped away her tears with his fingers.

"Kit, it's okay. Mellow out. We're up here. The hammerhead's down there. We're safe. You can relax."

"I know. I know we're safe, but somehow I still can't really believe it."

Eric pulled her closer, then put both arms around her and lowered his lips to hers in a gentle kiss. She wasn't surprised to find herself kissing him in return. Ever since that first kiss on the beach at the Marquesas, she had imagined what kissing Eric again might be like. Heaven. That's what it was like.

Then she pulled away. He was only kissing her to

comfort her, kissing her as her father might kiss her when she was hurt or frightened. But Eric was still holding her hand, and when she tried to ease from his grip, he tightened his hold.

"I've wanted to do that for a long time, Kit."

"You have?" She couldn't help the surprise in the voice, the doubt.

"Yes, I have."

"What stopped you?" It was a blunt question, but she needed the answer. She didn't want kisses of pity or compassion from him. She could do without that quite easily.

"Surely you must know what stopped me. I knew you and Rafe were an item. I didn't want to cause trouble."

She felt warmth begin to seep into her at last. "Me and Rafe? Me and Rafe an item?"

"Looked that way to me that morning I saw you having breakfast with him at Casa Marina. And you were at the dock with him."

"Rafe and I are just good friends. He had a sort-of job for me, and I was just easing out of it, telling him about our charter business." She laughed ruefully. "It's you and Dian who are the item, I guess."

Eric looked at her in surprise before he grinned. "You really mean that, Kit? You really mean you thought—"

"What else could I think?" Kit had wanted to speak of Dian for so long that the words fairly poured forth now that Eric had given her the opportunity to speak. "I've seen you with her at the dock. I've seen her waiting for you in your car at the marina. I'm not blind. I've seen how you talk and laugh with her as if you've been friends forever.

You speak so casually of entertaining her in your home for dinner. What else am I to think?"

Eric looked at Kit with a very serious expression, with no trace of laughter. "You might try thinking that Dian's my sister-in-law. Dian Hartley. Mrs. Henry Hartley."

Kit could only stare at him as she tried to digest the news he had given her.

"Didn't you hear me introduce her that day at the treasure exhibit? Dian Hartley—Henry's wife. They've been married three years."

Kit felt heat rush to her neck, rise to her face. "I'm sorry. I mean I really thought you had about the neatest girl friend a guy could have. She's so accomplished and . . . and . . ."

"And she's twenty-six years old, Kit. Even if Dian weren't married to my brother, she wouldn't give a kid like me the time of day."

"She looks younger."

"I know, but she's twenty-six. She's out of college, and she's been into her career for several years."

"She looks younger." Kit felt like a broken record. What must Eric be thinking of her!

"Enough about Dian, Kit. But what about Rafe Mira? I've seen you with him several times. McDonald's. The dock. Casa Marina. And he seems to be on exceptionally good terms with your parents. At least I presume your dad wouldn't trust the mo-ped keys to a stranger, would he?"

"I guess I can understand why you might have gotten the wrong idea about us."

"I thought you were steadies, especially since you kept reminding me of our business relationship. I took those words as a friendly warning to keep my distance in matters that didn't pertain to our charter business."

Kit began to smile and relax. Thoughts of the recent shark attack began to fade into the background as she concentrated on Eric and the misunderstandings that had controlled their thoughts and their actions.

"Rafe is just a good friend, Eric. That's the truth. He and Anita and Dave and I hung out a lot last year. Then the car crash sort of pulled us more closely together."

"I can understand that. You were survivors."

"Right. And the surviving gave us a lot in common. When it was clear that I wouldn't be working for gramp this summer, Rafe tried to help me out with a job of distributing flyers for a condo. But we're nothing more than good friends."

"Well, now that you and I are also survivors, I hope we'll be just as good friends as you and Rafe." Eric looked at her with a warm smile. "Maybe even better. We've survived a shark attack. We just had a very close call."

"I know. You saved our lives, Eric. You were very brave down there."

"Not really. The sea bass was the thing that really saved us. If it hadn't come along when it did, we might not be here right this minute."

Kit couldn't speak. She felt weak, but at the same time, she knew a sense of peacefulness, a sense of understanding Eric that had been lacking before. Dian Hartley. The name sang through her mind. Dian Hartley. Mrs. *Henry* Hartley. A relative. Not a girl friend at all. A relative.

"Are we going back to Key West now?" Kit asked after they had rested for a while longer. "It's really getting late in the afternoon."

"We could carry a few more stones," Eric said. "I hate to go in without as many as the *Starfish* can carry."

"Eric, I have big news for you. I'm not about to dive down there again today. That shark might return."

"I suppose you're right. There's blood in the water."

"Right. Some other shark might smell it and come to pay a visit. No more diving today."

"I forgot about the blood. We'd be crazy to risk going back in now." Eric counted the stones in the bottom of the boat. "Forty. We'll take these to the Rusty Anchor for starters, and maybe we can come back tomorrow and bring up more."

They headed toward Key West. It was dusk before Eric moored the *Starfish* at the dock in front of the Rusty Anchor. The pelicans sitting on the pilings, looking like wise grandfathers, winked at them as they passed, but they made no effort to fly away.

"They're probably expecting a handout," Kit said as she walked on tiptoe in her deck shoes, trying not to limp. "Too bad to disappoint them. Ballast stones won't make a very good meal."

She and Eric left the dock and headed for the café. Greg had many customers, but he took time to talk with them for a few minutes.

"Forty, eh?" he asked.

"Want to take a look at them?" Eric asked.

Kit could hardly believe that Eric wasn't going to

tell Greg about the shark attack. How could he keep
it to himself! It was so big in her own mind that she
knew she would blurt the whole story to the first
person who acted as if he would listen to her.

"Sure, let's take a look," Greg said. He followed
Eric and Kit to the dock and examined the stones in
the bottom of the boat. He just stared at them for a
brief time; then he picked up one of the stones and
hefted it in his hand.

"Just think, kids. The last person to touch this
stone was probably some Spanish sailor who lived in
another age and time."

Kit grinned at him. "The last person to touch that
stone was either Eric or me."

"You know what I mean," Greg said. "They're
old. They're a part of history."

"Maybe since they're so historical we've underes-
timated their true value," Eric said. "Maybe they're
worth a lot more than a mere two bucks each."

"No way." Greg grinned at them. "A deal's a
deal. Let's get them out of the boat."

"What about your customers?" Kit asked.

"You kids can carry them to the anchor and pile
them around the base of it," Greg said. "I may work
out some fancy design with them later, but for right
now, just toss them down near the anchor."

"Right, man," Eric agreed. "But it's going to take
a while."

Kit sighed and felt embarrassed. Her leg was
beginning to ache, and she knew she shouldn't exert
it by toting ballast stones from the boat dock to the
front of the café. But she wanted to do her part of
the work.

"I've got a wheelbarrow," Greg said. "Let's wheel it onto the dock, load it up. I'll help you. They won't miss me inside for a couple of minutes. I've hired an extra man tonight."

"Good deal," Eric agreed. "We had a bit of a brush with a shark out there, man. Used up a lot of energy."

Greg studied them carefully. "Look, I don't want you kids taking big risks to bring me back a few chunks of stone. No way. No more going into shark-infested waters."

"The water wasn't exactly shark infested," Kit said. "There just happened to be this one big, huge hammerhead scouting around for a meal."

"And we were almost his meal," Eric said.

"What happened?" Greg asked. "How did you escape?"

"A sea bass came along, and while the hammerhead was chasing it for hors d'oeuvres, we made our escape." Eric grinned as if hanging out with a shark was nothing unusual, but he winked at Kit, and she felt a closeness to him that hadn't been there earlier.

"Sounds as if you lucked out," Greg said.

Kit wanted to tell Greg how bravely Eric had acted, but a certain look in Eric's eyes pleaded with her to remain silent. And she did.

"Yeah," Eric said. "We lucked out."

"How many stones you got here?" Greg asked.

"Forty," Eric said.

"Soon as we unload them, I'll write you a check." Greg left them, returning minutes later with the wheelbarrow. Kit sat in the boat and handed the stones up to Eric and Greg, holding to a position that kept her left leg relaxed. And once the stones were unloaded, she remained in the boat while Eric went to collect the promised check.

"Your leg's hurting you, isn't it?" Eric asked when he returned to the boat.

"A little. It'll be okay once I get home and get some heat on it."

"I'll get you there as quickly as I can," Eric promised. He took a direct route to the marina, secured the *Starfish* in its slip and then helped Kit onto the dock.

"Shall we stop in the office to see if anyone signed up for fishing tomorrow?" Kit asked.

"Later. I'll call out here after I get you home. First things first."

Kit held on to Eric's arm as she limped toward his car. It was good to know that Eric understood, that he didn't think she was a freak because of her leg. When they reached her house, he walked with her to the door, then paused.

"You going to tell your folks about the shark?"

"I don't think so," Kit said, secretly wondering if she could keep from telling.

"Maybe you should tell them."

"What good would it do? They might forbid me to go diving again."

"Maybe we should call off the deal with Greg," Eric said. "Even he said he didn't want us taking risks."

"No way, Eric. The sea is full of sharks. A person is more likely to die from a bee sting than from a shark attack."

"Where'd you hear that?"

"From gramp. He gathers statistics like that.

When he gets a customer who's shark shy, he brings out the statistics. It calms them down. Sometimes."

"Are you afraid to tell your folks?"

"Not exactly. I just don't want to worry them. We're safe. Like I said, the sea is full of sharks, and the only way to be sure of avoiding them would be to stay on land. I'm not going to let fear control my life."

"Good girl." Eric patted her arm. Then he brushed a light kiss against her cheek. "I've got a surprise for you, Kit."

She was so surprised that Eric had kissed her again that she could hardly speak. And now that they had their misunderstanding about Dian and Rafe straightened out, she knew he had kissed her because he liked her.

"Aren't you going to ask what it is?"

"What what is?" she asked.

"The surprise. I just told you I had a surprise for you." Eric sobered. "Hey, I'm really sorry. It's your leg, isn't it. You're really hurting, and here I am talking about sharks and surprises. You get on inside and take care of yourself. I'll talk to you later."

Kit felt trapped. She didn't want to tell Eric that his kiss had had such an effect on her, but neither did she want him to think that she was suffering on his account. "Hey, my leg isn't hurting all that much. It's just telling me to slow down a bit. Give. What's the surprise?"

"It's something you'll like, I think. I'll call you in the morning." He backed toward the porch steps, then turned and walked to his car, leaving her no more opportunity to speak of the surprise.

Kit walked on inside, but she watched Eric from

the window until he climbed into his car and drove away. A surprise. What could it be? She had had so many surprises that day, some good and some bad, that she needed time to go to her room and think about them.

She was glad her parents weren't home. It was their evening to grocery shop. She needed some minutes to herself to sort out new ideas, to sort out her feelings toward Eric. They were business partners. They were survivors. What else were they?

12

After taking a warm bath and humoring her leg for another half hour with the heating pad, Kit felt much better. At the supper table, she mentioned nothing about the encounter with the shark, but she did tell her parents that she had used her scuba gear and training to help Eric bring ballast stones to the surface.

"Are you sure they were ballast stones?" her father asked.

"Eric said so, and Dian, his sister-in-law, agreed. She's a marine archaeologist." How good it felt to say those words.

"Your grandfather will be pleased to hear about the find, Kit," her mother said. "Why don't you call him after we're finished eating and tell him all about it."

"Okay. I will."

"How many ballast stones were down there?" her father asked.

"Lots. Greg White, the owner of the Rusty Anchor, wants to buy two hundred of them, and there are lots more than that."

"A large pile of ballast usually indicates the spot where the main portion of a ship went down," her father said. "Timbers rot and wash away, and artifacts are sometimes carried far from the spot where the ship sank. But the ballast stones usually mark the exact place."

"How do you know all that?" Kit asked, surprised at the things her dad was telling her.

"Oh, I had a college course in ancient Spanish history, and I used to do some treasure diving now and then."

"You never told me," Kit said.

Her father laughed and pushed his chair back from the table. "You never asked."

"Did you find anything?"

"Not much. The Spaniards themselves salvaged most of the shallow water wrecks."

"That's what Eric told me."

Once Kit and her mother were finished with kitchen chores, Kit called her grandfather; they talked for almost fifteen minutes about the scuba gear, the diving and the ballast stones.

"The diving can be good exercise for your leg, Kit," gramp said.

Unless you meet a hammerhead. "Right, gramp. I'll bring you a ballast stone for a souvenir." Kit ended the conversation feeling that she had pleased her grandfather, which, in turn, pleased her.

That night, Kit pulled a fishing encyclopedia from

the book shelf and carried it to bed with her. She read about hammerhead sharks, and the information made her curious about other types of sharks. She knew only about black-tips and their feeding patterns on the flats. It surprised her to learn how many other kinds of sharks there were. It was almost midnight when she snapped off her bed light and let the encyclopedia slide to the floor.

But she didn't go to sleep. She had too many things to think about, to wonder about. She had missed Nita that summer. That was for sure. But in a way her mother had been right. She was beginning to really think for herself. It surprised her to know that she didn't feel totally lost without Nita's opinion on everything. But she did wish Nita were closer. She had some new things to tell her about. She didn't need her opinion. She just wanted to tell her, to share her thoughts.

Eric didn't call the next morning. He stopped by in person. And Kit was dressed and ready to leave the house. What was his surprise? She could hardly wait to find out, but she was determined not to act like a little kid at a birthday party, begging to see a gift.

"How's the leg?" Eric asked as Kit joined him on the front porch.

"Fine. Why did you wonder about that?"

"I could tell yesterday that it was really bothering you even though you made light of it. You get a certain look in your eyes, a certain tightness at the corners of your mouth."

Kit didn't know whether to be pleased or exasperated. She didn't want Eric to treat her like an invalid, but on the other hand, she was flattered that he had noticed such small details. She decided to be pleased, and with the decision came the flash thought that most of her happiness or unhappiness was a result of her own thinking, her own choices.

"I gave the old leg the heat treatment when I got home, and it's fine today." She walked with him toward his car.

"I've got some great news, Kit. There's a couple coming here to house sit for a friend while he's visiting up north, and they've booked the *Starfish* for every day next week. *Every day!*"

"Eric! Why didn't you tell me yesterday? That's great. Super great!"

"I didn't know about it yesterday. At least not when we were together. The call came in late last night."

"Then that isn't the surprise you mentioned?"

"Well, it's a surprise, all right, but it isn't the one I told you about yesterday."

"Eric! Aren't you excited about the charter? Someone must really have put in a good word for us."

"Right. And guess who?"

"Can't."

"Maggie McGinnis," Eric said. "The Gordons, that's the new couple, said Maggie McGinnis recommended us."

"Neat! Really neat!"

"It's more than that. It'll secure my first semester at college. Room, board, tuition. The whole bag. And if I can find a job at the university that might pay my room and board, this week's charter could secure my whole freshman year."

"That's great," Kit said.

"And it means you can buy the boat you've been wanting," Eric pointed out.

Kit hesitated. "Maybe so."

Eric didn't say where they were going, but he headed toward a marina that carried a line of small boats. He parked the car, then came around and opened the door for Kit.

"Why are we stopping here?" she asked.

"I want to show you something. Henry put me onto it, and I think you'll be impressed."

"What is it?"

"Guess."

"You're buying a new boat?" Kit asked, but she knew that would hardly be the case.

"I'm not buying a new boat, but I thought *you* might be." He led her inside a shed where many boats were on display. Walking slowly past a row of small fishing crafts, he paused before a turquoise and cream-colored model and pointed to the price tag.

"Here it is, Kit. This is the one Henry was telling me about. It's here for consignment sale. The owner is moving up north, and he wants to sell it quickly. At this price, it's a steal. I thought you might be interested."

"Eric! It's beautiful."

"Agreed. I wouldn't mind having it myself."

"Look at those lines! *Pelican Pete*." She read the name stenciled on the stern, and then she walked around the boat, studying it from all angles. "It's my color, Eric. Turquoise and cream. Sea colors."

"And it's already equipped with a poling platform, a fishing chair, even a pole." Eric touched the pole, turning it in the clamp that held it in place.

Kit closed her eyes for a few seconds, picturing herself in *Pelican Pete* on the flats, the sun shining, the onshore breeze up just enough to cool her cheeks.

"Hey, you all right?" Eric touched her elbow.

"I'm fine." She opened her eyes and smiled up at him. "Just dreaming."

"You don't need to dream about it, Kit. With your savings and the charter coming up next week, you can have this boat if you want it. It's a *steal* at this price." He reached into his pocket and pulled out some bills. "By the way, here's your share of the money from the ballast stones. And there'll be more to come as soon as we make another delivery to Greg."

Kit took the bills and poked them into the pocket of her jeans. "Thanks, Eric." Then she turned her back on *Pelican Pete*. "And thanks for showing me the boat. It really is a beauty. Henry knows how to spot them."

"You want to talk with the owner about it?" Eric asked. "I can get his name for you."

"No. No, I don't think so." She wanted to look back at the boat, but she didn't. If she looked back, she might give in. "Would you mind driving me by the bank, Eric?"

"Sure thing. Need to stop by there myself." He drove the short distance to Key West First National and parked in the customer's lot across the street.

Kit smiled at the armed guard inside the entrance of the bank and walked to the teller's window. Picking up a deposit slip, she quickly filled it out, laid the bills Eric had given to her on top of it and pushed it toward the teller. When she had received a copy of the deposit slip, she turned and joined Eric, who had finished his business and was standing near the door.

"Going to build up your boat account a bit before you make a decision?" he asked as they strolled back toward his car.

Kit kicked a twig along the pavement and sighed. "It isn't a boat account anymore, Eric." They settled themselves in his car before she continued. "I've been doing a lot of serious thinking here lately."

"About what?"

"About the future. About the past. I've decided that I'd better plan on enrolling in college after I am graduated from high school. I've decided that I *want* to go to college."

"That's a switch." Eric grinned at her. "Give."

"You're teasing me."

"Not really. I'm just surprised. You seemed to know exactly where you were going, and I'm surprised you've changed your mind about it."

"You're the very first person I've told, Eric. I mean I haven't even told my parents yet. In fact, I guess I just decided for sure when I saw *Pelican Pete*."

"When you saw *Pelican Pete?* A boat changed your mind? You're full of surprises, Kit."

"The boat changed my mind along with a lot of other things. You helped change my mind, too. You and Dian and Greg White and a hammerhead shark and—"

"Hold on a minute. You're losing me."

Kit swallowed around the lump that threatened to

block her throat, and she blinked back tears, tears for a boat she might never own, a life she might never lead. "I've got a lot to learn, Eric."

"Don't we all!"

"I mean I've been so in love with fishing, so intent on making charter fishing my way of life, my career, that I've overlooked a lot of interesting things."

"Like what?"

"The sea has many faces."

Eric remained silent, and after a while, Kit continued, sorting out her thoughts as she spoke. "I've got to face the fact that I may never be strong enough to be a full-time charter-boat captain. That kind of a life may work out for me, but then again it may not."

"That's true, I suppose, if you really face the facts of the matter."

"Lots of kids can't decide what they want to do with their lives once they're out of high school, but I think that maybe I decided too quickly."

"So what else do you have in mind?" Eric asked.

"I'm not sure. But I need to know more about Spanish history. Your chatter about ancient Spain and her treasure galleons fascinated me. I couldn't get them out of my mind. And then I learned that my dad had been interested in them at one time, too."

"I didn't know that."

"You can talk to him about it sometime. He said he'd done some diving on wrecks of the old galleons but that he hadn't found anything."

"So you're going to be a treasure diver?" Eric asked.

"No. I don't think so. But Dian's career as a marine archaeologist attracts me, too. And so does underwater photography. That might be something I'd like to do, something that I could do. Swimming strengthens my leg. Right now I can move easier in water than I can on land."

"Dian would be glad to tell you more about her work," Eric said. "It's not hard to get her started."

"I want to talk with her. And Greg White and his shell collection fascinates me, too. And all those tiny fish in his aquarium. I'd like to know more about them. And about sharks. Suddenly, it seems as if the whole world has opened up to me, letting me see things I've been blind to before."

"I'd like to forget about sharks," Eric said. "They're nothing but bad news."

"Last night, I read about hammerheads and about other types of sharks, too. You know, there's a lot scientists don't know about those creatures. There are lots of blank spots, and there are a lot of people doing research on the subject."

"So you want to be a researcher?"

"Eric, there are so many things I don't know enough about, so much that I'll never find out about in high school, that the only solution seems to be to go on to college. From now on, I'm thinking of that money in the bank as my education fund."

"Sounds like a good idea to me," Eric agreed.

"The way I look at it, the money will buy me time as well as information about things I need to know."

"Time?"

"Sure. In four or five years, I'll know for sure just what my physical capabilities will be. By that time, I'll have investigated lots of career possibilities. I'd love to have that boat, Eric. I want it so badly I can almost taste it. But I can't afford it."

"Of course you can afford it, Kit. The money's in sight. The price is right."

"No. I can't afford it. I can't afford to limit myself to a career choice that could go right down the tubes if my leg doesn't develop as I hope it will."

"Oh." Eric held her hand, gave it a squeeze.

"Don't look so glum, Eric. I won't have you feeling sorry for me. No way. Let's go home and celebrate."

"Celebrate?"

"Celebrate my decision. I'll make you the biggest key lime pie this side of Miami."

Eric laughed, but he started the car. "Key lime pie at this hour of the morning! You think I'm an addict or something?"

"Right. I do."

They drove back to Kit's house, and the telephone was ringing as they stepped through the front doorway. Kit hurried to answer it.

"May I speak to Katherine Cummings please?" a deep bass voice asked.

"This is she speaking." Kit held her breath. Who was this? Nobody called her Katherine. But nobody.

"This is Paul Johnson calling on behalf of the Key West Teen Tournament. We're happy to inform you that you have won first place in the black-tip shark division of the tournament."

"That's wonderful!" Kit exclaimed, hardly able to realize that it was July already, that the tournament had ended. "I mean, that's really wonderful!"

"Congratulations," Mr. Johnson said. "The tournament banquet will be one week from today. Will you be present to receive your trophy?"

"Yes. Yes, of course I'll be there."

"Will you be needing extra tickets for friends and family?"

"Uh, can I let you know a little later? I mean, I'll have to talk with . . . some people."

"That will be all right. Just get your reservations in before next Tuesday."

"Fine," Kit said. "And thank you again for calling." She replaced the receiver and stood staring at the telephone, unable to move or to speak. She had won! She might never have the strength to fight a big fish again, but this one time she had done it, and she had won her division of the tournament.

She turned from the telephone, wondering if she should tell Eric. She remembered their hard words at the rehab clinic. Eric had wanted to win, too. What would his reaction be? Since they had started their business, there had been little time for pleasure fishing. Maybe she would say nothing right now. Plenty of time to tell Eric later. Much later.

"So you won the tournament," Eric said when she turned to face him.

Kit felt her mouth drop open. "How did you *know?* I mean, you couldn't have known."

Eric smiled at her and took her hand. "I knew that nothing else could leave you speechless and staring at the telephone. Congratulations, Kit. Congratulations!"

"Thanks, Eric." She studied his face as she felt the warmth of his hand, trying to read his eyes, his mouth, trying to tell if he really meant what he said.

"There's just one thing," Eric said, looking her straight in the eye.

Kit gulped, but she said nothing, and she noticed that he was still holding her hand.

"As a loser in the tournament, I think you owe it to me to attend the banquet with me. How about it?"

"Oh, Eric! Do you mean it? I was afraid you'd . . . Oh, I'd love to go to the banquet with you." She kept looking at him, half afraid he might withdraw the invitation.

"There's just one more thing," Eric said, again looking her straight in the eye.

"What?"

"Right now I'm expecting the biggest key lime pie you've ever made."

"Coming right up." Reluctantly, Kit withdrew her hand from his and opened the refrigerator. Limes. Eggs. She opened the freezer. Pie shell. And from the cupboard she took condensed milk and a mixing bowl and mixer. She hoped Eric hadn't noticed that her hands were shaking. "It'll be a masterpiece, Eric."

"There's just one more thing," Eric said.

Kit paused. "What?"

"Kiss me, Kit." In the next moment, Eric was pulling her to him, kissing her gently but thoroughly. And she kissed him back, enjoying the moment. That was all anyone ever could count on, wasn't it? The moment. *Kiss me, Kit.* The words sang in her mind, and she listened to them, memorizing their melody.

First Love from Silhouette

THERE'S NOTHING QUITE AS SPECIAL AS A FIRST LOVE.

$1.95

24 ☐ DREAM LOVER Treadwell

26 ☐ A TIME FOR US Ryan

27 ☐ A SECRET PLACE Francis

29 ☐ FOR THE LOVE OF LORI Ladd

30 ☐ A BOY TO DREAM ABOUT Quinn

31 ☐ THE FIRST ACT London

32 ☐ DARE TO LOVE Bush

33 ☐ YOU AND ME Johnson

34 ☐ THE PERFECT FIGURE March

35 ☐ PEOPLE LIKE US Haynes

36 ☐ ONE ON ONE Ketter

37 ☐ LOVE NOTE Howell

38 ☐ ALL-AMERICAN GIRL Payton

39 ☐ BE MY VALENTINE Harper

40 ☐ MY LUCKY STAR Cassiday

41 ☐ JUST FRIENDS Francis

42 ☐ PROMISES TO COME Dellin

43 ☐ A KNIGHT TO REMEMBER Martin

44 ☐ SOMEONE LIKE JEREMY VAUGHN Alexander

45 ☐ A TOUCH OF LOVE Madison

46 ☐ SEALED WITH A KISS Davis

47 ☐ THREE WEEKS OF LOVE Aks

48 ☐ SUMMER ILLUSION Manning

49 ☐ ONE OF A KIND Brett

50 ☐ STAY, SWEET LOVE Fisher

51 ☐ PRAIRIE GIRL Coy

52 ☐ A SUMMER TO REMEMBER Robertson

53 ☐ LIGHT OF MY LIFE Harper

54 ☐ PICTURE PERFECT Enfield

55 ☐ LOVE ON THE RUN Graham

56 ☐ ROMANCE IN STORE Arthur

57 ☐ SOME DAY MY PRINCE Ladd

58 ☐ DOUBLE EXPOSURE Hawkins

59 ☐ A RAINBOW FOR ALISON Johnson

60 ☐ ALABAMA MOON Cole

61 ☐ HERE COMES KARY! Dunne

62 ☐ SECRET ADMIRER Enfield

63 ☐ A NEW BEGINNING Ryan

64 ☐ MIX AND MATCH Madison

65 ☐ THE MYSTERY KISS Harper

66 ☐ UP TO DATE Sommers

67 ☐ PUPPY LOVE Harrell

First Love from Silhouette

68 ☐ CHANGE PARTNERS Wagner

69 ☐ ADVICE AND CONSENT Alexander

70 ☐ MORE THAN FRIENDS Stuart

71 ☐ THAT CERTAIN BOY Malek

72 ☐ LOVE AND HONORS Ryan

73 ☐ SHORT STOP FOR ROMANCE Harper

74 ☐ A PASSING GAME Sommers

75 ☐ UNDER THE MISTLETOE Mathews

76 ☐ SEND IN THE CLOWNS Youngblood

77 ☐ FREE AS A BIRD Wunsch

78 ☐ BITTERSWEET SIXTEEN Bush

79 ☐ LARGER THAN LIFE Cole

80 ☐ ENDLESS SUMMER Bayner

81 ☐ THE MOCKINGBIRD Stuart

82 ☐ KISS ME, KIT Francis

83 ☐ WHERE THE BOYS ARE Malek

84 ☐ SUNNY SIDE UP Grimes

FIRST LOVE, Department FL/4
1230 Avenue of the Americas
New York, NY 10020

Please send me the books I have checked above. I am enclosing $_____ (please add 75¢ to cover postage and handling. NYS and NYC residents please add appropriate sales tax). Send check or money order—no cash or C.O.D.'s please. Allow six weeks for delivery.

NAME _____

ADDRESS _____

CITY _____ STATE/ZIP _____

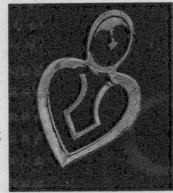